D0329377

a haunted heart

John MacKenna was born in 1952 in Castledermot, County Kildare. He currently works as a senior radio producer for RTE in Dublin. He has won a number of awards for his writing, including the *Irish Times* First Fiction Award for *The Fallen And Other Stories* (1992). He has also written another collection of stories, *A Year of Our Lives* (1995), and the novels *Clare* (1993) and *The Last Fine Summer* (1998). He lives in County Kildare.

Also by John MacKenna in Picador

a year of our lives

the last fine summer

JOHN MacKENNA

a haunted
heart

PICADOR

First published 1999 by Picador

This edition published 2000 by Picador
àn imprint of Macmillan Publishers Ltd
25 Eccleston Place, London SW1W 9NF
Basingstoke and Oxford
Associated companies throughout the world
www.macmillan.co.uk

ISBN 0 330 35275 X

Copyright © John MacKenna 1998

The right of John MacKenna to be identified as the
author of this work has been asserted by him in accordance
with the Copyright, Designs and Patents Act 1988.

All rights reserved. No part of this publication may be
reproduced, stored in or introduced into a retrieval system, or
transmitted, in any form, or by any means (electronic, mechanical,
photocopying, recording or otherwise) without the prior written
permission of the publisher. Any person who does any unauthorized
act in relation to this publication may be liable to criminal
prosecution and civil claims for damages.

1 3 5 7 9 8 6 4 2

A CIP catalogue record for this book is available from
the British Library.

Typeset by SetSystems Ltd, Saffron Walden, Essex
Printed and bound in Great Britain by
Mackays of Chatham plc, Chatham, Kent

This book is sold subject to the condition that it shall not,
by way of trade or otherwise, be lent, re-sold, hired out,
or otherwise circulated without the publisher's prior consent
in any form of binding or cover other than that in which
it is published and without a similar condition including this
condition being imposed on the subsequent purchaser.

for Lydia MacKenna

Thursday, April 2nd 1959

*

When the train rounded the curve at the end of the station, moving away to Maganey and Carlow and the other stops on the Waterford line, and the steam cleared from the platform, I realized just how hot today really was. The trembling carriages and melting cloud left a heat in their wake that collapsed onto the afternoon. At the other end of the empty gravel walkway a porter furled his green flag and sauntered towards me, leaving my trunk where it had been unloaded from the baggage compartment. I stood, a travelling bag on either side, acclimatizing myself, summoning the energy to speak.

'Good afternoon,' the man said. 'You're welcome to Athy. Is there someone to meet you?'

I shook my head.

'Do you need a hackney?'

'I need to have my bags delivered. And the trunk.'

'That can be done,' the man said. 'Where to?'

'Offaly Street. Number five.'

He nodded.

'Miss Miller's place, Lord rest her.'

'Yes,' I said. 'I'm her cousin. Elizabeth Hallhead.'

1

'Not too many of that name about here.' The man smiled.

'No.'

'You're English yourself.'

I shook my head.

'I've lived there for the past sixty years but I grew up in Ballitore.'

'Ballitore.' He weighed the idea for a moment before laughing. 'Aye, well we all have our cross to bear.'

I laughed, too.

'I'll get these bags sent down. It might be half an hour, the cart is out delivering.'

'That's fine,' I said. 'It may take me that long to get there myself.'

'You know the way?'

'Unless the town has altered radically in the last sixty years.'

'Devil a bit. Not in fifty-four, anyway, I can vouch for that.'

'I'm sure I'll find it, then.'

'Right,' the man said, lifting my bags and walking up the steps to the parcels office. 'Well, enjoy your stay.'

I made my way through the narrow gate to the side of the footbridge and onto the roadway in front of the station house.

Immediately, the smell of lilac soaked the air and a laburnum showered over the low wall at the side of the house, golden rain, the only rain in weeks. Further along, flowering currant dripped through a wire fence, onto the bonnet of a black Morris Minor.

I crossed the road and walked through the park, climbing the polished steps onto the street, and I knew exactly where I was. Surprised myself with the clarity of my memory. Across that road, down a flight of steps outside the Railway Bar and along the empty street towards the town square. And, halfway there, I remembered another detail. There should be a lane, somewhere to the left, a lane that arched back onto the square. And there it was. Meeting House Lane. I followed its camber and came on the closed Meeting House, dead behind its iron rails. I thought of the young woman who had sat opposite me on the train this afternoon, the woman whose neck was white as our smocks had been, whose hair was tied back tightly, as their mother's was when we stood outside that Meeting House, sixty years ago. The young woman who, for an instant, reminded me of their mother.

And then I moved on, crossing the square between the dilapidated Town Hall and the Courthouse, to the banks of the River Barrow where Joshua Jacob had urged people to be baptized into the numbers of the White Friends. While I stood there, a confetti of cherry blossom fell straight in the still air, and I had some sense of the fate that conspired to bring me back here, of the need to tell the story. To tell them the truth about the mother who was scrubbed from their young memories. To let them know the cost of her desire.

So, when I've settled here, in my new and temporary home, when I've begun the process of patching up my own mortality, I'll do my best to put those missing parts of their lives together again. There's a chance that they'll resent my interference, that what was lost or buried is best left that way, but I do this for the three of them – Lydia, Myfanwy and Abigail. Maybe, most of all, for Abigail. If there's any part of her soul in theirs, and surely there must be, then they'll want to hear what I have to tell.

I found the house, my cousin's house, and met, at last, Mrs Murphy, who has corresponded with me since Ruth's death, this woman who has been the single thread tying me to the life and death of my cousin. Before coming here, I often felt I knew her better than I did Ruth and, of course, that's true. Ruth was not born until the year after I left this country and, in spite of all our correspondence over the past twenty years, as last surviving cousins, we never met.

But Mrs Murphy's letters have been of a different kind, full of news about the town, herself and this house, urging me to come and see it, to know what it was I'd been left and what I might be losing if I sold it without visiting.

The welcome that awaited me, this afternoon, was genuine. The tiny yard was spick and span, filled with the colour and the smell of early wallflowers. The house clean as a new pin, the windows open to the heat outside. The back bedroom, which I have taken for my own, looks down over a gaggle of derelict cottages, slates elbowing the bleached rafters to make room for saplings that poke their heads. Beyond these, a meadow of sculpted cattle chew the cud, the sun glazing their coats, and beyond that again the slow waters of the Barrow.

Mrs Murphy tells me the mornings are full of the songs of birds.

'You won't sleep long past five, I'll tell you that. Ruth never did. None of us do. You'll hear nothing of the street and everything of the birds at that hour.'

Well, we'll see.

In the end there were so many things conspiring with fate to bring me here – inquisitiveness, illness, age, mortality, memory. Memory least of all but memory will take advantage of the others.

I'll put my time to ordering the journals from sixty years ago, prepare the story for Lydia and Myfanwy. More than that I cannot do.

Friday, April 3rd

*

I need not have worried about the birds for I hardly slept a wink. I've always been like that in new surroundings. But how right she was! The heavy curtains which withstand the light from the morning sun are no protection against the lunacy of the birds in the trees and bushes behind the yard.

I lay awhile, going back over yesterday's journey, visualizing the young woman on the train. Seeing, again, the sensuous crescent of her neck, where it curved beneath the path of her taut hair. Imagining how that line travelled to her shoulder and traced its way to the arch of her breast. Imagined how beautiful that breast must be, how soft, how hard. Like Abigail's.

But the memory went and I left my bed and dressed. I'd breakfasted by six. Then I set about taking stock of the house.

It's crammed with furniture. The furniture that Ruth collected and added to the pieces her parents and grandparents had stuffed into rooms.

I took note of what I might need here and, when I thought the hour respectable, called on Mrs Murphy and her husband and asked them to choose any pieces they might like. The rest I'll sell. I grew used, over the years, to a more disciplined order in my various accommodations and have never felt the absence of unnecessary furniture to be an austerity.

Mrs Murphy has arranged for a local buyer to call tomorrow to take away what she and I don't want. I feel no sense of loss about the things that will go. Instead, I look forward to brighter, less cluttered rooms. Rooms where there is space to move about.

'When you shift that lot, you can open up a dancing school,' Mrs Murphy said.

I spent the afternoon pottering about the town, enjoying the sunshine and finding my bearings again. It's not a difficult town to negotiate. Built in a cross that intersects on the market square, there are few places to go astray. The lanes that run off these main streets inevitably find their way back again, making it impossible to get lost.

This evening, I sorted out the few contents of my travelling bags, hanging my dresses, laying out the remainder of my clothes in the drawers in my bedroom. I was thorough, in Kent, in throwing out anything I didn't need. That much of Joshua Jacob's philosophy remains. Tomorrow, when the furniture man comes, I'll put a table in one of the front bedrooms and have him bring the trunk up there. Then I can set about what I now regard as my business.

Tomorrow, too, I'll take my letters and notes to the doctor and introduce myself. Not that I expect miracles.

We left the miracles behind when we were young women, Abigail and myself. My concern is more with survival now and less with living.

Wednesday, April 8th

*

The house has begun to take on something of my personality, I think. I've weeded out a great deal of the clutter. What furniture the Murphys liked I insisted they take and I was quite brutal in clearing the rest. The furniture man came back a second and a third time to remove what I didn't want. I think he was quite pleased with what he got and I was satisfied with what he paid. I went out on Saturday and bought a phonogram and I've put this in the upstairs room which has now become my study. In all my years, there were so many houses in which I worked where there were book-lined studies and now I have my own. Not book lined, and not likely to be, but a place where I can write my account of our lives together. I have a table there, a scrubbed deal table taken in from the back yard, and a comfortable chair, my phonogram and records and my trunk of journals. I feel quite privileged!

The room is shaded from the sunshine so I need not be distracted by the days outside.

Through the weekend, with the Murphys' help, I put order on the other rooms so that now there's space to move about and I'm not greeted by a dark mountain of mahogany each time I open a door.

Yesterday, my bicycle arrived on the train, faithfully following me from Kent. If all goes well enough I can, at least in the coming weeks, rediscover some of the places we went together. Much depends, the doctor says, on the rate at which this illness progresses. I like to think of it as 'this' rather than 'my' illness, that way I keep it at arms' length.

He told me on Friday that the signs were good, that it had taken so long in developing that it might continue to move slowly.

'If we can control the pain then there's no reason why you shouldn't go on enjoying life,' he said.

He's a pleasant young man. We discussed music, though he had never heard of Glinka or Nicolai. But then, as I accepted, I knew nothing of the music that interested him. Local music, jigs and reels and the like. He did, however, seem intrigued to meet someone who had grown up in a Quaker household in Ballitore.

'Are there any Quakers left there now?' he asked.

I told him I didn't think there were.

'I'll cycle out and see,' I told him.

I think he thought I was joking until I assured him I had pedalled my way through much of England in my holiday times.

'Well, don't overdo it,' he warned.

'But you're not telling me not to do it?' I asked.

'Certainly not. If you feel well enough, do it.'

I considered asking him how long he believed I might

be able to go on cycling and how long after that I might have a fair degree of health but I knew he'd not give me a straight answer, even if he could.

Monday, April 13th

*

I woke on Friday morning to the sound of the birds but there was another sound, too. It took me a while to recognize the noise of rain. Torrential rain. It cracked and lashed against the corrugated-iron roof of the shed in the yard.

By lunchtime, it had washed the tiredness from every leaf in sight. The laburnum and blackthorn and lilac and sycamore and elm were much more sprightly. The slates on the rooftops shimmered, cleansed of their grit.

In the afternoon, the rain eased but it didn't stop and it has gone on raining all through the weekend and shows no signs of easing. People say the farmers need it, I'm sure they do, but I have become quite depressed. What if this rain goes on, if we're to be lumbered with a summer so wet that I'm confined, more or less, to this house? What if the months slip by and there's no sun or light or dryness to get out and cycle to Ballitore or Levitstown, places I want to see again? What if the weather stays down until my strength is gone? That thought torments me. The thought of having to take a hackney car, to travel as an invalid to the places I wish to visit on my own. I'd dared to imagine myself getting to these places under my own steam, investigating them at my leisure. I'd even gone so far as to see myself pedalling home under a full moon. Reliving. What a pleasure! To relive the past, to be there alone with time on my hands, to have time to forget that, in truth, there's so little time. But now, with the sun gone, the house is dark and disturbing. God knows how Ruth survived here through the winters with the shadows of great, dark furniture massing like clouds in every corner of the rooms.

I've tried to force myself to set to work. What better opportunity, I tell myself, what better chance to get the thing started? And I will but I wish the sky would crack just long enough to let some sunshine through, to prove that summer hasn't passed us by in spring's disguise.

Wednesday, April 15th

*

This morning, in spite of the melancholy drizzle, I took all my journals out of the trunk and arranged them, year by year. My life in sixty-nine journals. The sight might have depressed me but once the books were there I became quite excited at the prospect of reading again the accounts I had not read in decades.

I allowed myself the afternoon to dip in and out of my simple, childish entries from that first year, when I was ten. So much there about my grandfather Hallhead. Even then, even before I could express it in writing, I was perplexed by how a man so warm, so loving, so willing to laugh, could have produced a son as dreary and joyless as my father was. No surprise that he married a woman as grey as himself. Some surprise that they managed to produce me, I shudder at the incongruity of the idea of their lovemaking. The sodden shirts, a foot apart on the clothes line in Murphy's yard, seem an appropriate metaphor. Such sights make me all the more grateful for the fifteen years my grandfather was with us. I remember the liberation of his company, my secret wish that he had been my father, the longing for my parents to go away and leave my grandfather and myself to our wilful ways.

Even now I marvel at the excitement he engendered in the mundane – in a walk to Mullaghmast or a journey to a Quarterly Meeting in Carlow. The most ordinary things were crammed with possibility. Wasn't that the energy that I found, again, in Abigail? The ardour that accepted nothing less than abandon in return.

I think of my grandfather, almost as old then as I am now, taking my hand and launching us out from a towering rick of straw to a lower one, twenty feet below. There was no consideration of the possibilities of injury, just the impetuosity of the moment. And so it was with Abigail.

Thursday, April 16th

*

I spent most of this wet morning and all of the afternoon beginning my account for Lydia and Myfanwy. The habit, over the years of housekeeping, of copying every list that I made or every instruction I gave or was given has prompted me to make a copy of the document in this diary. Why? Vanity. I don't think so. The hope that someone will one day read it? I'm not sure. Will it matter if it's read?

I'd like to think so but, probably, it won't. Anyway, this is what I have to tell, or the beginnings of it.

*

I first met your mother, Abigail Beale (née Meredith), in the February of 1899. You were three years old, then, Lydia, and you, Myfanwy, were two. But before I tell you of that, I need to step back a short space, to the first time I saw Joshua Jacob, for he was to be the one who brought your mother and me together and the one who caused the separation between you and your mother.

Late in the month of January 1899, a stranger appeared at Meeting for Worship in Ballitore. He was a tall, bearded man and he spoke at length about the way in which Friends had drifted from the ideals of the founders of Quakerism. He was particularly scathing

*about the creeping luxury which he perceived in Friends'
lives.*

*He arrived that morning, dressed soberly in black hat,
coat and britches, and seated himself on the edge of a
pew. Meeting had not long begun when he rose to speak,
his huge frame moving awkwardly.*

*I recall quite clearly what he said, for it made a great
impression on me then and I was to hear it repeated
many times in the months that followed.*

*'We have surrounded ourselves with luxury, as though
we can hide behind curtained windows and flamboyant
clothes. As though our saviour, Jesus Christ, will not
recognize us in this ludicrous garb.'*

*He looked about him, holding all of us hostage to his
eyes, allowing us to wither in his silence before continuing.*

*'Christ tells us to knock and the door will be opened.
Do we think, therefore, that Christ cannot knock and
open the doors of our houses, cannot enter at will, cannot
mount our stairways in the dead of night or the light of
day and see us for what we are, as we are?'*

I blushed at that thought.

*'Do we think Jesus Christ cannot see what things are
written in our hearts? And when He sees, is He not
stricken at the sight of such foppery? There can be no
salvation for those who profess the one and practise the
other. Professing meagreness while living amid plenty. No
salvation for those who do not turn their hearts to the
simplicity that was part of Friends' lives.'*

He paused again, drawing up his shoulders, breathing deeply and exhaling, before whispering in a voice that was low and cold.

'No salvation.'

None responded to his challenge and, afterwards, as my mother and I made our way home, I asked what she had made of his outburst but she would not be drawn. I assumed she was not impressed by his words and was all the more surprised when the man appeared at our table for lunch.

His tone, in the familiar surroundings of our dining room, was more conciliatory. He explained that he had left his business in Dublin, a thriving tea importation enterprise, in the care of his wife, Sarah Fayle, and set off to preach to Friends across the country. In his months of travelling he had, however, met with little success and had determined that if Friends were not to be led from within they might be troubled from without.

'It is my intention to establish a new Society,' he told us. 'A commune of people who will return themselves to the ways of the early Friends, to the plain way of speaking and thinking and living. I will find a place where we can live that simplicity.'

'Will you find those willing to follow?' my father asked. 'I see the good sense and the necessity of what you say. But I cannot see where you will find those willing to follow you.'

'I already have disciples,' Joshua said quietly and he smiled at me. 'And there will be others. The numbers do

not matter, all I ask are pure hearts and souls that have not been lifted up to vanity.'

How do I explain to you the effect this man had on all of us? I was not particularly impressed by his words. They were extreme, of course, but they did not have a particular attraction for me. It was more the certainty of Joshua Jacob himself. His obvious faith in what he was saying, a belief that would brook no opposition. If he could not convince from within then he was prepared to step outside. This, to an eighteen-year-old who had experienced only the most dreary of lifestyles since my grandfather's death, offered possibility. And when he looked at me I knew I would go with him because he offered escape.

I tell you this because I want you to know how attractive life seemed when Joshua Jacob spoke. What he offered was a chance to return to simplicity. Life is simple when you're young. That was the appeal to me.

For your mother there was a greater allure, attention and warmth and love. Commodities that were in short supply in her marriage.

I don't propose this as an excuse for her leaving you, merely as a reason why she was prepared to countenance that thought in the first place. There was, too, the perceptible ardour she had for Joshua. I doubt I can do that justice, I only hope you find some hints of it in this history.

Friday, April 17th

*

This morning, just after six, I rose and made some tea and sat in the kitchen, reading what I wrote yesterday. It falls so far short of what I'd hoped. It's bland and flat. I doubt they'll want to read beyond the first paragraph. Why should they? It tells them nothing of the way things were then, the way we were. It doesn't even begin to push open the door on that time and those events.

How do I tell them about the things that have stayed with me? The overwhelming presence of Joshua Jacob; the loveliness of their mother; the rigour of her husband, their father; the danger that surrounded our lives, so far beyond the pale of acceptance that had we stopped to think we might all have lost our nerve. In the end, it was Joshua, the strongest, who proved weakest in this regard. Others might say Abigail was the weakest of all, that she surrendered completely, but I don't believe that. What she did was done because she was the only one who refused to compromise in any way.

And me? Had I loved her as much as I believed I loved her, should I not have followed her to the end? Did I not betray her as much as her husband had done, as much as Joshua Jacob did? I protest that my concern was a comfort to her but I may be lying to myself. How do I explain that to her daughters? Maybe this whole thing is a mistake, a silly attempt to justify the thoughtless.

Monday, April 20th

*

How much can happen in a day, how much can change between morning and evening!

I visited Dr Fullard this morning, to collect a prescription. He seemed pleased with my condition. I felt much better than I'd done before the weekend. The sun reappeared on Sunday and I put my improvement down to that fact alone.

We discussed the importance of sunshine on the spirits.

'You were surer of sunshine in the south of England than here, you know,' he said.

I agreed.

'But music can be every bit as uplifting,' he added, opening a press and taking out a case from which he produced a set of gangling pipes.

'Uilleann pipes,' he explained. 'When I play these, I forget the weather and the world and the troubles I deal with every day. These are my wings.'

'And why do you keep them in your surgery?' I enquired.

He grinned, sheepishly.

'My wife won't let me play them in the house. She says the sound reminds her of a cow with her tail caught in a gate. Isn't that encouraging?'

I like Dr Fullard very much. He has an openness about him that reminds me of William Ackworth.

In the afternoon, when the sky had been wiped clean of clouds, I took out my bicycle, packed some sandwiches in the basket and set off for Ballitore. I took the Castledermot road but missed my turn at Foxhill and had to retrace two miles of my journey. But I didn't mind. It was good to be cycling again, perched on my bicycle, looking over the whitethorn ditches into fields clustered with cowslips. I felt the life flooding back into my blood. I allowed myself the luxury of imagining how Ballitore might look and how I might approach our old home.

Some miles along the road, I stopped and sat on a boulder by a gateway to a forest. As I ate my sandwiches, I estimated it had been two months since my last bicycle journey, which explained the aching joints.

And then the clouds came, scudding in across the treetops. In a matter of minutes, the day darkened and the wind rose, strapping rain from the east, while the sky fell. I tried to push the forest gate open but it was bolted and padlocked and too high for me to climb. I cursed my age. The ditch on the other side offered nothing in the way of shelter while the rain tunnelled down the roadway, chipping my face and soaking me in seconds. Across the murk of the sky I couldn't find a single crack that offered even the possibility of dryness. There was nothing for it but to start cycling back the way I had come, back the miles I had relished on the outward journey, my legs aching as I tried to hold a steady line in the teeth of a gusting wind. Turning into Athy, off the Castledermot road, a watery sun glared from the wet tar, blinding me.

I held my tears in check until I was safely back inside the house and then they came. I saw myself in the hall mirror, old and drenched and out of energy, and I cried. I stood at the foot of the stairs, sobbing. To be old, to be alone, to be so foolish as to think I can recapture any part of the past. How arrogant! How stupid!

Wednesday, April 22nd

*

Yesterday morning, Mrs Murphy arrived with a freshly made rhubarb tart and stayed for almost four hours. It was as if she sensed what I'd gone through the previous day. We drank pots of tea and she talked about Ruth and about neighbours and about times for not being there and being there and the importance of knowing the difference between the two.

'Neighbours are neighbours,' she said, 'or you might as well be living up in the Rushes.'

After she'd gone, I went upstairs for something and looked out through the back window. A black kitten was playing in a yard, three doors down, launching itself through the air, grabbing onto a dress on the clothes line, swinging, holding on for dear life before dropping to the ground and starting all over again.

And, later still, the man on the radio talked about showers giving way to sunshine. Maybe it's another conspiracy but it worked. There was the possibility of my clothes drying out, of a neighbour who wanted to be that and no more or less. I even dared to imagine summer coming back to haunt us until late October. All these good hopes conspired to sit me down, after tea, and take up the story where I'd left it off.

*

I broached the subject of joining Joshua Jacob's group with him that Sunday afternoon in Ballitore.

My father had asked me to show Joshua the village and we were walking the low road, past the Meeting House, down to the drained pond at Shackleton's mill.

'My grandfather used to take me out there,' I told him.

'Where?'

'There. It was drained about ten years ago. When I was a small girl it was a tiled pond. My grandfather

would take me out in a boat on summer evenings and we'd lie there, listening to fish plopping around us.'

'You were fond of your grandfather.'

I laughed.

'I adored my grandfather.'

'To find such love is a good fortune. Such simple love.'

As we turned, to walk back home, I asked him if I might join his group.

He didn't seem at all surprised, it was as though he expected my question.

'And your parents?' was all he asked.

'I'll speak to them.'

'I will be in Carlow on seventh-day for Meeting, if you wish to meet me there. There are others joining me then. We will travel to Mountmellick and look for a permanent place to live, a home of our own.'

That night, I lay awake, wondering why I had presented myself to be one of Joshua's followers. It had something to do with what he offered, I couldn't deny that, but it had more to do with a need to escape from my parents and the monotony of life in Ballitore. I had no idea what Joshua might offer but I doubted it could be any more trying than the terrible ordinariness of day swallowing day in our household.

I spoke first to my father and, like Joshua Jacob, he showed little surprise at my request.

'There's much to be said for what Joshua preaches,' he said. 'And I can see the attraction his words hold for the young. But you're ill-prepared for such a life,

*it will be difficult and basic. I have no objection, in prin-
ciple, but I worry about your ability to survive the
rigours.'*

'But you don't have any scruples about his message?'
He shook his head.

*'Then let me try,' I said. 'You can't and Mother can't,
your lives are tied to your business and this house, but
I may be the one to go in our name.'*

And so he was persuaded.

*My mother dithered a while but she would not go
against my father and, five days later, I took my leave
of Ballitore and set off, with my father, for Carlow where,
on the following day, I met, again, with Joshua Jacob.
There, too, I met those followers he had gathered. William Ackworth – a young man in his twenties; James
Stubb – a middle-aged man to whom I took an immediate and abiding dislike; and George Carr, an elderly
man who had been a minister of the Church of Ireland
but was now committed to the new ideas.*

*After Meeting in Carlow, I said farewell to my father
and heard Joshua promise he would return me to my
parents should I find the new lifestyle not to my liking.
We spent the remainder of that day travelling, by cart,
through Athy and Maryborough and on to Mountmellick. We arrived there, cold and tired, to find an ardent
welcome, a good meal and a blazing fire to greet us. All
were the work of John Wickham, an old man who was
to become a firm friend of your mother and myself. He
was a man devoid of any malice. His fervent interest was*

in gardening and this, more than all the words and opinions and texts, brought outsiders to our door when, finally, we settled in our home.

But, in that, I am skipping ahead. In those dead days, at the end of January, we were five men and one young woman living in community in Mountmellick. Preparing ourselves for the warmer days when we would go out into the market place and preach the word of God.

At that time, Joshua was clear on some of the doctrines by which he believed we should live but he had not yet begun to have his 'openings', the trances from which he would emerge with messages from God as to what we should do and how we should live.

My first days in Mountmellick were lonely ones but the friendship of John Wickham and William Ackworth and George Carr made them bearable.

It was in the earliest days of that February I first saw your mother, Abigail. She came to a meeting in Mountmellick, in the company of her cousin. There were others there that night, Friends from Mountmellick and Portarlington and Maryborough – we all still regarded ourselves as Quakers then. Your mother was the only one from Rosenallis. I had only heard of the village before then and the name had always fascinated me.

After Joshua had spoken, as we drank tea and chatted, I mentioned this to Abigail.

'That was exactly how I felt when I first went to Rosenallis,' she said. 'I thought it the most beautiful name in the world. When our first daughter was born I wanted to call her Rose but my husband wouldn't hear of it. I told him we could call the second girl Alice. All he said was: "What if we have a boy?" That was that. And in the end we had another girl.'

I asked about her daughters and when she spoke of you she became exhilarated. This is true. She was suddenly vivacious, animated, spilling out your names and the tiniest details of your infant lives.

Did you know, Lydia, that early in the January of that year, when your mother opened the door on your first snowfall, you stood there, enchanted, before turning to her and exclaiming: 'It's as deep as a goose!'

And did you know, Myfanwy, that you were the only one in your generation to have your grandfather Meredith's blue eyes? That gratified your mother.

Those were the things she told me on that frozen evening in the winter of 1899. Yours were the first names on her lips. Your every quip and accomplishment was a source of pride and pleasure to her. Only those of us who saw the depth of that pride and heard the love in her voice can know the heartbreak she endured. And it was not something she could easily show.

Abigail would talk and listen and advise any and all of us, when she joined our community, but there was nothing she could say or do to soothe the awful grief inside herself.

I know that when she left us that night I felt as though I had made a good and close friend, someone I would long treasure. I didn't know then that Abigail would *become a member of our group. Nor did I know the strength of feeling that was growing between her and Joshua Jacob. Later I recognized the roots of that emotion and realized they had been sown in the indifference that already existed between your mother and father. But none of this was known to me on that first night.*

*

Have I said enough in that? And how much do I tell them of the strength of feeling that existed between their mother and Joshua? She was passionate about him and must have felt his affections were the same, though I never saw him – but once – express himself with the fervour shown by Abigail. Still, there were signs enough there in the things he did and in the way he put their love before all else when he was first put to the test. That's what made his subsequent actions all the more unexpected and painful.

*

There is no doubt about the strength of feeling that grew between your mother and Joshua. And it grew so quickly! Had it progressed more gradually, things might have been different for Abigail and for you. But such was the ferocity of events, public and private, in the months of that spring and summer that there was no opportunity for anyone to be impartial, lines were drawn before we knew it and no one would budge. You won't remember any of that but my only hope is that, when you read this, you will find yourselves able to escape whatever disapproving attitudes you may have held towards your mother.

*

It's difficult to know what tone to take in writing this. Whether Lydia and Myfanwy were instilled with an attitude of loathing towards Abigail. I can only hope they have, at least in equal part to their father's bitterness, a good share of their mother's generosity.

Thursday, April 23rd

*

Maybe, instead of all this, I should bundle up my journals from that summer and give them to them, if they can be located.

This morning, I sent off an enquiry to Friends in Dublin in the hope of tracing Lydia or Myfanwy. Best to know they are alive, if I'm to continue this. All I could give were their names and dates and place of birth. Even if they are alive they may not be Friends any longer. All I can do is hope. Or do I hope? Would I be happier to know they are beyond my reach, not to feel responsible for being the one to bring them face to face with a past they may not welcome?

Monday, April 27th

*

After a weekend of warm, dry weather, I woke this morning to another blue sky and a strong sun. The radio forecast confirmed what daylight offered and I set off again for Ballitore. I have to confess to looking over my shoulder more than once on the journey but the day remained clear and kind, warm but with a pleasant breeze.

I stopped at the forest gate – tempting fate? – and enjoyed the sunshine while I rested. The road from Athy to Ballitore is longer than I remembered but once I caught sight of the rooflines of the village I found new strength in my legs and sped downhill, butterflies in my tummy. It struck me that I hadn't been in Ballitore in this century – I didn't come back for my parents' burials. Ruth had overseen those and the sale of their house. My only connection with the place had been occasional letters back and forth and the arrival of a cheque in 1935, the proceeds of the sale of the house, after my father's death. And now here I was, back again when all were safely dead and buried.

Stopping on the deserted corner, where one street rose to the height of the Dublin–Waterford road and the other angled away to the Meeting House and my old home, I was faced with the ruin of Leadbeater's house which, in my childhood, had been a hive of activity.

I turned right and cycled slowly, keeping my eyes on the ground, nervous of seeing what was become of the place I was born. Only at the last moment did I look up, into the empty doorway of dereliction. Three floors of broken windows under a roof that's still more or less intact.

I propped my bicycle against the gable wall and stepped in through the doorway, into godforsaken dilapidation. No furniture remains but the open fireplace in what was once the drawing room. There are no rooms any more, only the bones of the place. Rafters and splintered floorboards hanging askew, the ground floor littered with twenty or thirty years of neglect.

Through the gaping back door, the garden is a wilderness. Flowering currant, sycamore, oak, roses, lilac, elm and every weed under the sun have run riot. I managed to push halfway down the long, narrow garden before their twisted plaits proved too much for me. I stood there in the sun, the smells of long ago drizzling from every branch. Then I went back and sat on the granite window sill of what had been our kitchen.

I remembered, clearly, as though I was back there and then, the afternoon in the autumn of my fifteenth year, when I left my grandfather sitting at the end of this garden, reading, while I rambled off to the Seven Trees Hill. My parents were away, otherwise I wouldn't have been allowed even that short walk without company. But I went with my grandfather's encouragement, his blessing even.

'Enjoy yourself,' he told me. 'Just get back by night-fall.'

I told him I would and I did.

Though it was to be four years before, finally, I left Ballitore, I think I left it that afternoon. And standing there in the garden today, disordered and all as it is, I could recollect it as it was then. The trees leaning in over the pathway that coiled to the lawn where my grand-father always sat when there was heat in the evening sun. And there was heat that late September afternoon. Heat and flurries of a west wind coming down off the high road.

I took my walk and stopped, on the way back, to talk to Mary McCormack and Paul Choiseul and T. J. Dug-gan and Lurlene Nevin. I remember every detail of that conversation. I could tell you what they wore. Every particular is burned into my memory, as though my mind sensed what was about to happen and knew I would want to recall these details in the years that followed.

And the particulars of the house are there, too. Dim-ness in the hall, a certain sadness about the kitchen, the door still open on the mild evening, dusk gathering in the garden. I think I knew, as soon as I came into the house, but I recognized the fact of death when I caught the first glimpse of my grandfather, sitting on the bench he had made himself, his book still open before him, the early leaves of autumn poised like scales on his shoulders. And one on his hair, an absurd russet cap on his white locks. He'd have laughed at that sight. But there was no light, no radiance in his eyes. Nothing. For the first time in my life I saw no laughter in those eyes, no smile of greeting on that mouth. In that moment, coming face to face with death, I recognized the terror of desertion, the abysmal deprivation that his absence would dig in my life. It was as though everyone I loved and leaned on had died. And, in a way, that's how it was.

I walked the length of the path and stood a foot from where he sat. The breeze lifted one of the leaves from his shoulder and dropped it onto the open book. I waited for him to brush the leaf away but, of course, he didn't. Instead, I leaned over and lifted the leaf and put it in my pocket. Then I turned and ran through the house, ran next door to tell Nan Clarke, called Frank Taaffe and David Walsh and watched while they carried my grandfather into the house and laid him out on his bed.

I remembered that so clearly, treasured it today, was loath to leave the place because of those memories.

When I did, I turned in the ruin of the kitchen and looked back down the garden and pictured my grandfather there, saw his face light up at the sight of me, watched his hand rise in a wave of genuine delight and affection.

And then, I left.

I stopped, again, outside the ruined Meeting House, stood in the sun and viewed another ruin. Then I cycled up to the burial ground and found his headstone immediately, his grave overgrown with anemones. Read the simple script. 'Edward Hallhead. 1810–1895.' Only then did I look at the stone beside his. The names and dates of my parents' lives. They meant nothing to me, nothing at all. How can that be? They did nothing wrong. Did their best for me, I suppose. I had no reason to reject them. No, I don't think I ever did reject them. They were simply cast off as soon as I was old enough to recognize that option.

Is that why I was so attracted to Abigail Beale, because she too had gone through that process of exclusion?

I know, if I looked in my journal, I'd find that leaf, the one I took from my grandfather's book, on the page dated the twenty-first of September eighteen ninety-five.

I left the burial ground with mixed feelings. Glad to have seen, again, my grandfather's grave. Remembering the afternoon of his burial, the crowds of people lining the green road, proof – if proof were needed – of his popularity. It was the biggest funeral, people said, since Mary Leadbeater's, three generations earlier.

And I had seen the plot where I will be buried, beside my parents. My father might have given up hope of my ever returning in his lifetime but he had assumed I'd want to be buried in Ballitore. In that much, he saw the future more clearly than ever I did.

I got back to Athy exhausted, physically and emotionally.

Today I saw the past and the future and, standing among the rows of stones in the burial ground, the fact was reinforced that there's so little difference between the two. And so little time and so little space in which to make our mark.

Abigail made her mark, tortuous and all as it turned out to be. It deserves recognition. Tomorrow I'll get back to her story, word or not on Lydia and Myfanwy. If only for her own sake, if only for that.

Tuesday, April 28th

*

In the early days of February, your mother called frequently to our house in Mountmellick. Once or twice your father called to collect her but he seldom stayed long and it was obvious that he did not hold us in very high regard.

The last time I saw him there was at the end of the second week of February. At that stage, Abigail had been to visit us on five or six occasions. I had not had the opportunity to talk much with her. She spent most of her time with Joshua. He told us she was considering joining us and he was instructing her in our beliefs.

Your father came to that house, for the last time, on a wet evening in mid-February. Your mother had been with us all afternoon, with Joshua in a small room at the end of the corridor that ran from the front to the back of the house. This was the room to which Joshua retreated while we went about our work.

Sometime after eight that evening, there was a loud knocking on the front door and John Wickham went to open it. I was in the hallway at the time and I saw your father enter. He pushed roughly past John, without a word of greeting. At the end of the hall, he hesitated and called your mother's name. When she did not appear immediately he shouted again and banged open the door to the kitchen. Finding only William Ackworth inside he barked at him.

'Where is my wife, tell me where she is?'

William looked at him and replied: 'If I knew who your wife was I might be able to help you.'

'You know my wife. Abigail Beale. You know her well.'

At that moment, Abigail appeared from the room at the end of the corridor.

Your father turned and bellowed at her that she had no right to be there, that he had spent the evening in search of her, that he would not accept her behaviour and that she must not come to the house again.

'This man is depraved,' he said, angrily, pointing to Joshua, who stood behind Abigail. 'I have made you a comfortable home and a good home. He would have me pull it down and live in penury.'

'Simplicity,' Joshua said.

'There is nothing simple about you,' Robert retorted.

With that he took Abigail's hand and pulled her after him, through the open door and down the steps to where his carriage sat.

I took her coat from the stand in the hallway and hurried after them into the street. As I handed her the coat she said: 'Tell Joshua I will be back.'

Your father did not respond but flicked his whip and set the horse running so that I had no time to speak at all.

*

The things I remember. Each time Abigail came to visit, Joshua would take her to the little room at the end of the corridor and spend hours there with her. He told us she was considering becoming a member of our group and he was instructing her in our beliefs. I doubted that. I'd been in the house several weeks by then and there had been little question of individual preparation or instruction for the rest of us.

I doubt there was anything more to their times together than talk but all of us were aware of a tension between them.

'She must be a slow learner,' George Stubb muttered

one day when Joshua and Abigail had been closeted together a full afternoon.

I jumped to Abigail's defence.

'Easy for us to talk,' I said. 'We don't have small children and husbands to worry about.'

'Nor likely to,' he sneered, arching his bushy eyebrows. It was a custom of his I grew to hate.

'If they were all to come and be of us, wouldn't that sort it?' John Wickham asked.

William shook his head.

'I think that most unlikely, John. Most unlikely of all.'

The other thing that sticks in my mind was Robert Beale's roughness on the night he came in search of Abigail. The way he pushed past John Wickham in the hall. John was a hard worker but he was a slight man and elderly and Robert showed no respect for him that night. He might easily have hurt the old man but he didn't care. I'd happily have put Robert Beale in the same boat with James Stubb and sunk it without trace.

*

In the days that followed that confrontation, Joshua Jacob took to spending long periods away from the house, leaving before dawn and returning after dark, often scratched and torn from walking in thorny places. At the end of a week he called us together and told us of 'openings' he had been having from God.

'I have been listening for the voice of God. I have wandered in search of the silence that would be deep enough

for me to hear and I have found it. The Lord is telling us which way we should go and what we must do and how we will be called.'

Those were his words.

Over the following days, Joshua outlined the things we would do, how we would dress, by what name we would be called and what God expected of us.

It was at this time we became the White Friends.

'We are the true Friends, true followers of the Light,' Joshua told us. 'Our path will be straight and lit by the grace of God.'

It was a time of great anticipation. We had spent a period in waiting and now things would happen. Our days were taken up with work and in reading the Testaments but our evening meals were the highlight of the day. Across the table, we listened and talked and planned and questioned. The waiting was at an end and our mission was about to begin.

From that time, we dressed only in white. It was my job to make simple linen smocks which we wore over our working clothes.

'The Light has shone on us and we will reflect the Light,' Joshua told us and his words had the ring of a message that had, indeed, come from God.

*

When I think of the excitement, it's impossible to describe. We were a community possessed and being so few made everything more important and immediate.

This was the new beginning and we'd been entrusted with the message. But it was more than a message, it was the truth. We were the chosen.

There was a responsibility and joy in that thought. Joshua had instilled this conviction but he cautioned us, too. He warned us against rushing out without preparation. For that reason, we redoubled our commitment to the Testaments.

'"He preached the word unto them and they came unto Him,"' Joshua reminded us. 'We must know the word before we preach it. If God has chosen us, we must make ourselves worthy of His choosing.'

And so we read and studied and prepared. Even when we left the house and walked to the shops in Mountmellick we did it with a new energy and a conviction that our very existence would change the world. What we didn't know was how little we could change about ourselves and our own nature.

*

About two weeks after your mother's last visit to the house in Mountmellick, Joshua dispatched William Ackworth and me to Rosenallis, with word that she should come and worship with us on the following Sunday.

He instructed us to tell her this was the first full Meeting of the White Friends and he would like her there. He also instructed me to bring a smock for her to wear when she came.

We drove to Rosenallis with mixed feelings. We were

filled with the optimism of believers but it was tempered by our knowledge of your father's distrust.

Rosenallis was, then, a hamlet in which little moved. Your father's shop was one of a few in a solitary street that rambled between the houses but it was the most prosperous in appearance.

Beside the house was a low wall, enclosing a garden that was, even in that bitter time of year, well tended.

William and I went into the shop. It appeared empty but was warm, a stove throwing heat from the end wall. And then I saw you two, sitting together on a sack of grain near the stove, a book open between you, your heads bent together, one convulsion of golden hair exploding into the other. You looked so enchanting. I've never forgotten that sight. Before ever I saw your faces, I knew you were beautiful.

As we closed the door, your father appeared and, in the same instant, you turned to look up at us.

We enquired for your mother and you, Lydia, were sent to fetch her, Myfanwy trailing behind.

When your mother emerged, she welcomed us with open arms, taking us through the storeroom and into the warm kitchen where she served us tea and fresh brown bread.

She moved with such ease, such assurance, and you followed her about, helping to set the table. When the tea was wet, you called your father from the shop and he came and sat with us and we talked about the weather and William commented on the garden and we passed a strangely ordinary ten minutes before your father returned to his work.

When he was gone, we delivered Joshua's message and handed over the smock.

'Tell Joshua I won't be there,' your mother said. 'I've given Robert my word that I won't visit Mountmellick for a month. We've been married five years and I owe him that much, though I believe it's all I can give him. I promised him I would leave a month before deciding my course. He won't have me associating with Joshua and I won't have him keep me from you. We've agreed our terms. For this one month.'

'And he won't come with you? To hear what Joshua is saying?' I asked.

She shook her head.

'Robert believes Joshua is a threat to the Friends. He says anarchy will befall those who follow him.'

'Well, then,' William said, rising, 'we should go and leave you. I wish you well. All of you.'

As we turned our pony and trap in the street, I saw you – the four of you – in the doorway, together, smiling.

*

That freezing day. Wrapped in our coats against the bitter wind on the road to Rosenallis. But with our white smocks pulled proudly over all. The air razoring our faces. Fear, if only we'd admitted it, not knowing what reception Robert Beale might offer us. And the unexpected warmth and homeliness of the shop. The

40

beautiful children. And that odd encounter. No hint of the harshness of our last meeting. I found that strangest of all. The appearance of normality and the possibility of anger at any moment.

But what I haven't written, can't tell them, were the words Abigail whispered to me as we followed William through the storeroom and back to the shop. She laid a hand on my arm and held me back an instant, only that, so that no one noticed.

'Tell Joshua I love him.'

So quiet, I wasn't sure I'd heard. And, then, a fleeting smile of confirmation. How do I tell them that? I didn't tell William, as we drove back, and I didn't tell Joshua, either. I couldn't.

I've written more today than any day for months.

Thursday, April 30th

*

This town is so far inland, so far from the sea, yet I feel as though I've been lifted and dropped by waves. And not from that small sea between here and Britain. These waves seemed to have the strength of the Atlantic behind them. In the last few days, while I imagined only tranquillity, they were building. And then, without warning, I was lifted and battered and dropped and lifted again.

On Tuesday night I felt unwell but I put it down to the amount of writing I'd done that day. Yesterday, I woke feeling even worse. Nauseous and without the energy to get out of bed. So I stayed there all day, doddering in and out of sleep. But as night came on I couldn't do even that. So I got up and made myself some tea and toast. I came back to bed about ten but still I couldn't sleep. I sat in the big armchair all night long, looking out across the river, to the lights of the asbestos factory. A late cement train went up the siding and I heard the trucks lumbering and staggering. That was sometime after one. And that was when the pain began, burrowing through my stomach till I wanted to scream. I wondered if the Murphys would hear me if I did and if they'd come. I knew I couldn't get downstairs alone. Then the pain doubled me over so that I could hardly breathe, let alone cry out. And that's how it went on. All night. Coming in waves, battering me until I thought I'd die, wanted to die. I'd almost give up and then a break, loaning me a breath, giving me some ease, allowing me to hope it might have passed before it struck again. More pain, more breathlessness.

In the times between the agony, I kept thinking of what Dr Fullard had said, about controlling pain.

I cursed Ruth for not having had a telephone installed.

And that was how the night passed. I heard the quarter hours chime until just after four when, finally, the agony softened and I got downstairs. It was after six when I heard the Murphys raking out their range and I managed to get myself to their door and asked them to call Dr Fullard.

Credit where credit is due, he was down in less than ten minutes. He gave me an injection and I slept through most of the day. Any time I woke, Mrs Murphy was here. Dr Fullard came back this evening. He says I must take it easy and that he'll make an appointment to have me seen at some hospital in Dublin. As if I haven't been taking it easy. How much easier can I take it without giving up altogether? At least the pain is gone. For now.

Friday, May 1st

*

Who'd have thought I'd have welcomed summer as a crock? I feel better today than yesterday but only just. Mrs Murphy has been more than kind. Nothing has been too much for her and I'm set up like a lady.

Dr Fullard called this morning and, again, in the afternoon when surgery was finished. He won't, of course, say what, exactly, might be wrong.

'Leave it to the experts,' he said.

'I am the expert,' I told him. 'It's my body, my pain.'

He laughed but still won't commit himself.

'It might be something temporary, I hope it is.'

'Like life,' I said.

Wednesday, May 6th

*

Today is the first day I've been allowed outside. I spent the past week trying to persuade Dr Fullard and Mrs Murphy that I was fine. I'm not sure who took more persuading. I couldn't turn about without finding one or other of them there to suggest what I shouldn't be doing.

'I have to live,' I told them and the reaction was the same in each case.

Indeed I do but not without their organization.

The pain has gone but I'm to travel to Dublin tomorrow for tests.

My weekend case is packed and sitting in the hall.

I pointed out to Dr Fullard that I needed some exercise today if I'm not to be totally feeble for tomorrow's train journey. And so I made my escape from the house.

I walked down the banks of the river, to Ardreigh lock, and sat there a time.

The day gone by was splendid. The water irises are in bloom along the low water at the edge of Lord's Island. None on this side, of course. Faraway hills and all.

I've decided not to take my diary with me to the hospital. A little healthy superstition. A trust that if I leave it here I will return to continue it.

I'm seventy-nine years old. I've never been in hospital

overnight in my life before this. Should I be grateful or disappointed?

I was listening this evening to Vivaldi's Concerto in A Minor, the 'Largo Cantabile', when Dr Fullard called.

'What you need is some good "round the kitchen and mind the dresser" music,' he said.

Wednesday, May 13th

*

Lucky thirteen. I'm home again. Well rested and well tested. The Murphys came and met me at the hospital – how they knew I was for discharge they wouldn't say but there they were.

We travelled down by train and their nephew collected us from the station in his car and dropped us to the door and wouldn't hear of taking money. The house of course is cleaned and aired, with flowers in the kitchen and in my bedroom.

The hospital word is that there is no word, yet. The consultant told me he'll be in touch with Dr Fullard as soon as he knows anything. I can't say I was too fond of him. However, I may be glad of his services.

Now all I can do is wait. I hate waiting but I feel optimistic. Had there been anything badly wrong I wouldn't have been allowed home so quickly.

Thursday, May 14th

*

Today I returned to my account for Lydia and Myfanwy, though there's still no word in response to my enquiries about them.

*

Two weeks after our visit to Rosenallis, your mother appeared at the house in Mountmellick. She was in great distress. It emerged that she had told your father, the previous morning, that she was intent on going to Mountmellick and that it was her intention to join Joshua and the White Friends. At that news he forbade her to leave and, when she tried to do so, locked her in the storeroom.

Late in the evening, when you were both asleep, he freed her and tried to dissuade her from going but she told him she was determined to leave and to take you with her. At that, Robert threw her out of the house and she walked to Mountmellick. And so arrived, jaded, unsettled and afraid.

There was much to-ing and fro-ing in the days that followed. Your grandfather, Robert's father, came and spoke with Abigail, trying first to woo her back with promises and, when that failed, telling her she would never see you again.

Three days after this encounter, George Carr and I

*were dispatched to Rosenallis to try to talk to your father.
Why I was sent I have no idea. I spoke not a word during
the whole encounter. George was most conciliatory. He
had been a minister of the Church of Ireland, before following Joshua, and he was a good listener and a gentle
man.*

*I believe, in his heart, he wished to see your parents
reunited. Perhaps he knew, from the pain he had experienced in stepping out of his ministry, how hurtful the
times ahead would be.*

*

But had he known, had any of us, would we not – there
and then – have abandoned the whole enterprise?

*

*Our meeting with your father was long and intense. For
the most part, I concerned myself with you two. You
were unaware of the reasons for your mother's absence.
You were fascinated by the sight of George's white smock
and giggled when I asked if you would like to try it
on.*

*George used many approaches to your father – sug-
gesting that he might allow your mother to continue her
membership of the White Friends, in return for which he
would have her there with him. But he would not yield
on this.*

*'If she lives under my roof, she lives here as my wife,'
he said.*

'*You cannot make her be as you want in everything,*' George argued.

'*There are things in which we must be the same if we are to be man and wife at all,*' your father replied.

I believe each of us knew what the problems were – the lack of love between your parents – but none would put it into words and so the kernel remained untouched.

All this while, your mother continued in Mountmellick, fretting for you. I do not know what you have been told or what you may have imagined but the truth is that your mother was in deep despair at this time.

I cannot tell if her want of fondness towards your father or her commitment to the beliefs of the White Friends or her fascination with Joshua Jacob – or all three – drove her away from Rosenallis. But I do know it was not a lack of love for you. She could not stay where she was and your father would not allow her to take you with her. Indeed, he would not grant her any access to you at all. There was no choice in what she did. She must remain a prisoner or lose everything in fleeing.

Abigail was a woman of intense passion. I only wish that you could have known that passion. It was deeper than any I have ever experienced. Even when she had nothing left of herself, she gave to others. She gave when she might well have sought help. And she gave to you without your knowing it. That was the greatest pain. The love she suffered for you, day after day, directing it to where you lived and went about your young lives. Surely, you felt something of that intensity winging across the countryside, it must have found a place in your hearts and souls. I cannot believe otherwise.

But for her there was no way of knowing, only the hope that her love was reaching you. And only the tormenting knowledge that others who despised and detested her were in charge of your lives.

How often that crossed her mind, the thought that in spite of everything, in spite of the attempts she made to contact you, in spite of the heart that broke and broke again, in spite of love, there was no hope. And yet she went on living, smiling, loving all of us. In spite of everything.

Whatever pain you endured, be sure your mother endured an anguish a thousand times greater.

Friday, May 15th

*

Dr Fullard called this afternoon. He spent such a time beating about the bush that in the end I said to him: 'If you'd come in here with good news, you'd have told me straight away.'

'It's not bad news,' he said.

'Well, tell me, then. Spit it out.'

'It's more of the same. No news.'

'If you say "No news is good news", I'll do for you,' I told him. And I meant it.

So he told me. The tests have changed nothing. Simply corroborated what the tests in England suggested, what he suspected, what I knew.

'I know my own body,' I told him. 'We all do. And I'll know when it's run out of steam.'

And then I asked how long he thought I had.

'I'd say you have at least twenty-five years!'

I thanked him for his flattery and asked him how long the consultant believed I had.

'Six months,' he said. 'I hate this part of the work. Who knows? Any of us could be gone tomorrow. Who knows?'

'But he says six months?'

'Yes.'

'Well, then, we'd better hope for a good summer.'

After he'd gone, I cried. Of course I did. We can live with the uncertainty of life, with the tenuousness of daily survival but ask us to face the certainty of a time allotted and we find it impossible to do. Whatever the time it's never enough.

Wednesday, May 20th

*

Five days since I last wrote in this journal. Leaving one hundred and eighty or thereabouts. I've gone through all the mathematics. Four thousand three hundred and twenty hours. Two hundred and fifty-nine thousand two hundred minutes. Fifteen million five hundred and fifty-two thousand seconds. So much time. So little time. Such a waste of time.

Over the weekend, I tried to think but I couldn't think at all. Dr Fullard called, again, on Saturday and we talked practicalities. He suggested I have the telephone installed.

'In case of emergency.'

He told me it might take a little time but that he'd have a word with a couple of people and that it might speed things up. And then he apologized for not being straight with me on Friday.

I warned him not to tell anyone else, not to think a word in Mrs Murphy's ear might help.

'What if you need someone?' he asked.

'I'll have my telephone, won't I?'

'It's not the end, you know,' he said quietly.

I smiled and he blushed. To think I could make a young man, a young doctor, blush!

But of course it is. The end. Which is why I've spent the weekend and the first days of this week trying to think. Trying to find a way to live out this time.

On Sunday and Monday I considered tearing up the pages I've written about Abigail.

To hell with Lydia and Myfanwy, I thought, if they were interested in their mother they'd have found out the truth by now. If they can't be bothered, why should I?

But the more I thought about all this, the more I realized how few things I have to do, the more important this undertaking became.

When I questioned why I came back here last month, why I took this house, what the real reason was for wanting to return to Athy, there was only one answer. I came here to write Abigail's story and to try to find her daughters. To tell them. And not just because they should know but because I owe it to their mother. Many people took advantage of her – Robert Beale, her family, Joshua Jacob, Catherine Devine, me. None of them is living and none can undo what they did. I can. Perhaps that's why I was given this opportunity. Anyway, no more fractiousness. There's a story to be told and a time in which to tell it, so, yesterday, I wrote again to Dublin, enquiring about Lydia and Myfanwy. I need to get the story written. After that it's all a question of chance.

Yesterday, too, walking back along the river bank, in the sunshine, I remembered, out of nowhere, a Sunday in Ballitore. I can't have been more than eight. It was a hot day and we were in Meeting. I was seated by my mother and, looking out through the great, high window, I saw the sun oozing through the sycamore leaves and I thought, perhaps, God was not in our dull and gloomy Meeting room at all. Perhaps, He was out there in the trees, laughing. I whispered this notion to my mother. Clearly, she was appalled. Afterwards she scolded me. But my grandfather, when he heard the story, laughed and said he thought I had a very valid point and that no theologian could disprove it.

Why that came back to me I don't know but it made me smile and it warmed me inside where nothing else can warm.

I've just come to bed and opened this and reread it. Like a dream. A nightmare. Face to face with death. My death. The slow grinding down of the frail bits and pieces inside. Me. Growths, tumours, crock, cripple, chronic invalid. Afflicted, disabled, infirm, weak, dying. The rot, the graveyard cough. Sickbed, deathbed. Mine. This bed. This body. Bang, bang, bang at my front door. They're outside in the street, the undertakers, the auctioneers of life and death, doing their sums. If I can measure the minutes and the seconds, they can measure the turn on the stairs, work out how they might get my coffin down without removing the banisters. It comes to that. It's come to that.

Thursday, May 21st

*

Death is so many things. I thought I knew death. I've seen it, close up and distant, and thought I knew it. I believed I knew it better when I moved into its shadow, all those months ago, when it became a probability. But I knew nothing.

Death is terrifying. I wonder if it's shy?

The elders are in flower behind the derelict houses. I've sat at my bedroom window most of the afternoon, just looking at the trees and every so often my eye has been drawn to the open doors of those neglected houses.

Monday, May 25th

*

Yesterday was a good day. I woke feeling well. I ate heartily. The sun was shining. I wasn't conscious of deciding but something in me made the decision that I wouldn't feel sorrow or fear or pity. At best I'll live until I must die. At worst I'll be so ill that death will be a relief. In the meantime there's much to see.

Yesterday I went cycling. Didn't overdo it. Just cycled out to Levitstown, to where the White Friends once lived. I found the old mill and worked my way back to where our house had been but there's nothing left of it. I found the site but site is all it is. Still, I got there, walked about a little and got back home without distress.

And there was the kiss of the wind as I was cycling down the long, laggard fall into Athy.

And last night I slept soundly.

So, today, I set myself a timetable. To write in the

morning and enjoy the afternoon outside and write, again, in the evening.

*

The negotiations of those days had an intensity that is still fresh in my memory. Each visit from an emissary brought greater pressure on your mother.

There was no attempt among the White Friends to keep her with us. Many times William or I suggested to her that she should consider returning to Rosenallis but she would not hear of it.

'Those are my children. This is my life,' she'd say. 'I am entitled to have my children with me and they're entitled to my care.'

At one stage, at the end of February, your mother suggested, in desperation, that she might see a solicitor but Joshua would not agree to that. Friends, and more so White Friends, could have no truck with lawyers.

At the end of February of 1899, your father wrote a letter to your mother, a letter which I will give to you.

It was short and to the point:

*'Twenty-sixth day, Second Month,
Eighteen hundred and ninety-nine.
To Abigail Meredith –
Despite my best efforts there is to be no satisfaction of you. You have forsaken all that was dear to you. You have abandoned your babies in coldness. Your obsession*

has cost you all but bitterness and regret for the remains of your life. From this, Abigail Meredith is a harlot. Abigail Beale is dead and rotted.

Robert Beale.'

The day after this letter arrived, your mother set out for Rosenallis. She did not tell us where she was going but it was her intention to take you from your father's house. This she failed to do. He barred her from the house and you were kept inside.

The following day, the last of that month, Abigail, James Stubb and Joshua Jacob travelled to Rosenallis but, by then, you had been taken away to Dublin.

That night, Abigail persuaded James to return with her and daub much of the front of your father's shop with whitewash. The deed achieved nothing beyond hardening his resolve further.

The morning following this, your mother's father came to our house and sat with Abigail a good three hours. In the end, he told her he could not stand by her, that she had dishonoured her family and degraded herself.

As she saw him to the door he said, within hearing of all who were passing: 'I am bidding farewell to a stranger, neither you nor I have children any more.'

The scandal of all this did not go unnoticed, of course.

There were visits from a number of Friends from Mountmellick and Carlow and Athy but neither gentle chiding nor bitter words had any effect. When words failed, deeds were invoked.

On the third day of March we received a visit from the landlord of the property in which we lived. He gave us one week to vacate the house.

'This is a sign from the Lord,' Joshua told us. 'This is not the place we were meant to be. We will find a home where we may live simply and in peace.'

He and William Ackworth set out, the following day, to find us a new abode. They were gone four days and in that time I saw your mother languish. She was lost in isolation. Her children were gone. Her friends had deserted her. Her father had disowned her. She had been labelled a trollop by her own husband. The man to whom she had committed herself was away, promising a new home, but none knew where. Promises are little enough consolation in the face of such anguish.

I could do nothing for her. I was too young to have experienced anything of life. My only loss had been my grandfather's death and I had run from that when the first opportunity arose. That first day I followed her about, trying to engage her in conversation, trying to distract her, until John Wickham took me aside and said we should watch her but not interfere.

'There's no way into her heart,' he said. 'Even she can't find a way until it heals.'

*

John Wickham was a wonderful man. The more I remember of him, the more I admire his good sense and warmth. I regret not keeping in touch with him.

Everything about him was a comfort – his voice, his gentle way of doing things, his feel for the land.

Often, I've thought of him as a guardian angel to us all.

*

Late on the Sunday evening Joshua and William arrived back in Mountmellick, in the company of Joshua's wife, Sarah Fayle.

William explained that they had journeyed to Dublin on the day they left us. Having met Sarah Fayle they then travelled to Athy.

On the Friday, they located a property at Levitstown, halfway between Athy and Carlow, and by the following evening it had been bought by Sarah, for the White Friends.

We were to learn that Sarah and not Joshua was the business mind within their union.

She was a slight woman, looking older than her thirty-one years. Afterwards we commented on her sallow complexion and sunken eyes but on that first meeting she seemed a pleasant, quiet soul who knew what she was about.

She was aware of Abigail's state and was particularly attentive to her in the short time she stayed with us.

On that Monday, we packed our meagre belongings onto two carts and set off in the chilly morning air, away from Mountmellick, to our new home.

Joshua addressed us, just before we left.

'We are not going away because we have been forced, we are not going into exile. We have been in exile and now we are going home. "The captive exile hasteneth that he may be loosed." We have been loosed by God's grace.'

And so we left Mountmellick, on the ninth of March, 1899. Your mother never saw that town, her hometown, again.

Sarah Fayle travelled with us to Athy and then took a train back to Dublin. We journeyed on to Levitstown, arriving there as darkness fell.

Our new home was a long, low farmhouse, built on two sides about a square yard. On the third side were sheds and the fourth was formed by the roadside ditch and gate.

Inside, the house was spacious and uncluttered. Many would find it spartan but, coming from a cluttered home, I enjoyed the space it allowed.

An enormous kitchen took up most of one part. Off this was a small room that was to be Joshua's. A second bedroom was allotted to your mother and me. James Stubb and John Wickham shared a third and George Carr was given the fourth.

Ours was a comfortable room. The chimney from the kitchen range backed onto one wall, warming it in the coldest weather. We placed our bed against this wall and were snug as we could wish to be.

Beyond the bed, the room was plain – as were all the rooms – with two chairs and a chest of drawers. A long low window opened onto an orchard behind the house.

The kitchen housed a range, an enormous table, eight chairs and two long forms, a sink and more presses than I had ever seen. In the corner was a water pump. It was what Joshua believed it should be – simple.

Well tired with our day of travelling, we did little that night but eat a plain meal and retire.

As we lay in bed, I asked Abigail if she was all right.

'I will be,' she said but twice in the night I woke to hear her sobbing.

The next morning, our first in Levitstown, I spoke privately to Joshua. It was my first full conversation with him since I had joined the White Friends and I approached it with some reluctance, not knowing how he might respond. I warned him that Abigail needed help if she was to survive.

'I have been lax in seeing to her,' he said. 'Too many things have been thrown in my way. But I will see to her.'

I was relieved and gratified by his response, though afterwards, long afterwards, that phrase haunted me.

Nothing had been 'thrown' in Joshua's way that was not of his own making. But on that morning I was pleased to think he would accept responsibility for Abigail's recovery.

Wednesday, May 27th

*

Today I did something I've long wanted to do. I went to a circus. It was a small affair, tented in the field they call the Showgrounds. The tent was crammed with children but few adults. The afternoon was warm and overcast and I felt a little conspicuous making my way among the dozens of children but, once inside, I forgot my uncertainty and thoroughly enjoyed the entertainment.

It was a show where everyone appeared to do everything. The woman who sold me my ticket emerged, later, as a dancer. The man who took the ticket, at the entrance, was the magician. The woman in the mineral shop was a most talented tightrope walker. Clowns converted to bareback horse riders. It was an invigorating afternoon. I'd never before been to a circus and I'm pleased that I didn't allow my reticence to stop me.

Sitting in the warm tent, with the particular smell of the grass and the continual din of the children, I was reminded of our times as performers of another kind in the White Friends. The excitement of the children brought me back to the markets and fairs at which we preached and it gave me an appetite for continuing my account.

*

Joshua Jacob did talk to your mother in those first days at Levitstown. They spent much time together and her disposition improved greatly. It was a time of coldness and darkness and we were confined to the house for most of the following weeks.

Our time there was put to good use, making the house a most comfortable home and preparing ourselves for the days that were coming.

Joshua promised that we would set out, once the weather became milder, and travel to markets and fairs and events in the towns about us and preach the word of God to those who would listen.

'Our own brethren, those closest to the word, are deaf to the message of the Lord. They are the stony soil on which nothing will grow. We will search for a more fertile soil among the people on the streets.'

The thought of preaching in public filled me with dread but George Carr said it was a simple task.

'Speak in the expectation of being listened to,' he told us. 'If you once give a sign that you don't believe what you are saying then people will sense that and you'll lose their attention.'

'Easy for you,' Abigail told him. 'You had them nailed in their pews. We're preaching to passers-by in the street.'

'It's the same principle.'

'I'll remind you of that,' she laughed. 'Those words will haunt you.'

And so we prepared, with humour and trepidation.

The rains fell steadily through that month and we found it difficult to be in each other's company all the time.

Only John Wickham seemed impervious to the weather. He was constantly about the yard, fixing and hammering and taking every moment of dryness as an opportunity to get out and work the garden.

He and Joshua had drawn up a plan for developing the ground but all of that was to alter.

Once, in that period, Joshua was called urgently to Dublin where his wife had taken sick but she recovered and in a day or two he returned to us.

In the last week of March, Joshua spent several days away from the house. He set off on foot and did not return at night. We had been warned that he would be gone but there had been no talk of where he was going or why.

We were seated at table, eating supper, when he returned. The kitchen door opened and a figure was blown in on the wind and torrential rain. I hardly recognized him. His clothes were sodden and dirty, his beard plaited with mud. He sat a long time at the fire, saying nothing. We fed him soup and bread and then he went to his room and closed the door.

Once or twice, the following day, William Ackworth looked in on him but he was fast asleep. It was late in the evening before he reappeared. He had washed and cleaned himself and we saw, despite the inclement weather, that his skin had been tanned by the wind and open air. He was dressed in his white smock and looked quite striking.

*

It was, in fact, Abigail who spent all that day fretting, checking and rechecking that Joshua was still breathing. At one point, James Stubb turned on her.

'Leave him be, woman,' he snapped. 'Let the man sleep, can you not keep your foostering mind on the work you have to do.'

After that, she was more prudent and only checked when she and I were alone in the kitchen. I'd see her through the half-open door, looking down at Joshua's sleeping figure. All the energy of her love was in that look.

*

On the first Sunday of April Joshua rose during our Meeting and addressed us.

He talked about the time he had spent away from the house and why he had gone.

'Before, when the Lord opened to me, I listened and I brought His words to you. In the last days I felt His power breathing in me again and I went away to hear Him. He has told me what we must do.'

We waited, hanging on the word of God.

'We will be the White Friends. We will dress in the raiments of light. We will carry the word of the Lord to all who would hear and even to those who would not.

Those who have been shown the light and have turned to darkness will be known among us as the Black Friends, the Lord has told me so. Their darkness is the darkness of Satan. So the Lord has told me.'

He was silent, allowing the message to lodge in our heads.

'For those who have been shown the light and ignored it there will be no time. For the White Friends, who love the law, the law will be love. I bring this commandment, as Jesus brought it, that we love one another. We will live in a new light and a new life and the old ways will fall from us. The Lord has told me so. We may find His word beyond our understanding but we will rely on His mercy and His truth, for He has chosen us. He gave us this house, He blessed us with a life of simplicity and we must be simple in our obedience. Everything is known unto the Lord and ours is not to question but to do.'

Again, the silence that ensured we had time to take in what was being said.

'Here, in Levitstown, the Lord has given us a home. Here we will set our roots and from this place we will follow the steps of the Lord. We will preach, we will pray, we will live in love, we will be workers in the vine-yard of the Lord. We will plant a new vineyard here in His name and its wine will be His wine. The Lord has told me that we will drink of the cup that He drank of and be baptized with the baptism that He was baptized with.'

We did not realize, until later in the week, that Joshua meant literally what he said.

On the Wednesday following this meeting, he and John Wickham took the cart and drove to Athy. There they collected vines that had come by train from Dublin. That day, John set about preparing the ground and by the following Saturday he had set the poles and strung the wires and planted the vines.

This was done in the sheltered part of the garden, between the rear wall of the house and the high ditch of lilacs that separated us from the fields beyond.

This work was willingly undertaken. All of us were drawn by the image of our own vineyard. In the young vines we saw a metaphor for our own lives. We would grow and flourish and the fruit of our growth would be of consequence.

*

Wherever Joshua went that week, there Abigail went too. They were constantly in each other's company, their heads bent together, her face rapt. The affection between them was manifest enough to draw a constant grumble from James Stubb.

'Is there not a better way to praise the Lord than by gawping into that young hussy's eyes?' he exploded one afternoon.

'Woe to the scandal-giver,' William Ackworth said and there was something in his tone that James Stubb could not ignore.

But we all saw what was plain to be seen, the affection that was between them.

And, at night, in bed, there was nothing on Abigail's tongue but talk of Joshua, every conversation found its way to his name.

'"If we love the law, the law will be love." The Lord has blessed us with love. Our love is His blessing.'

'You mean your love of Joshua?' I'd tease.

'I mean the love all of us share. And the love between me and Joshua, and you and Joshua, and William and John. All of us.'

'But mostly you mean the love between you and Joshua.'

She blushed, when I said that, and smiled.

But who was I, who were any of us, to deny her that passion? Had she not well paid for it already?

*

When the vines were in, at the end of the first week of April, the weather lifted and cleared. The days were warm and there was no frost in the night. John Wickham set about working the rest of our land. William and James were put to working with him. Your mother and I looked after the house – cooking, baking, washing, whitewashing the rooms when the time allowed.

Joshua moved between us, sometimes working in the garden, sometimes sitting in the kitchen writing, sometimes retreating to his room.

Whenever he was with us, your mother blossomed. In

him she had found what she had never known in your father. I cannot put it more or less straightforwardly than that.

Two of the great turning points of our lives came in that month. Firstly, we went, as a group, with Joshua to Carlow to preach at the market there.

The night before our excursion, Joshua and William collected a large box from the railway station in Athy. When they returned, it was placed on the kitchen table and we stood in anticipation as Joshua opened it and took out a handful of pamphlets. On the covers, in bold letters, were the words:

'The Faith & Beliefs Of The White Friends.'

We cheered when we saw this. We knew then that we mattered, that we were not merely some splinter from another group. We were the White Friends.

That night, by candlelight in our room, Abigail and I pored over the eight pages that Joshua had written. There was no doubt about what he believed. We were chosen and those who had been offered the opportunity of redemption and had rejected it came in for his particular contempt. I imagined Friends in Ballitore and Athy and Carlow reading what he had written and bracing themselves against us, even before we met.

The following morning, before we left for Carlow market, Joshua gave each of us a bag filled with pamphlets. These we were to distribute to anyone who showed any interest in our beliefs.

Only John Wickham remained at the house. Joshua,

William, James, George, Abigail and I travelled by cart,
the six miles to Carlow.

The town was thronged and the great numbers of
people seemed to make Joshua more animated than I had
ever seen him. He was filled with nervous energy, urging
us on as we moved through the streets, looking constantly
about him until we reached the market area where, at
once, he lifted his voice above the clatter and gabble of
the crowd, calling them to hear the word of the Lord.

Our unusual garb had already caught the attention of
many passers-by and the sight of this tall, bearded
preacher quickly drew a crowd about him. William and
George stood one on each side of him. Abigail, James
and I distributed the pamphlets. Many people refused to
take them from us but many were interested and a few
stopped long enough to question us. At first, we were ner-
vous in answering but, as no one challenged what we
said, we grew in confidence.

And so the day passed. Joshua preached late into the
afternoon, until the market sellers began to dismantle
their stalls and the town and country people drifted
away. Only when the place was almost empty did he
stop his talking.

We travelled home that evening, the horse trotting
slowly, no one speaking. We were exhausted but we were
satisfied. We had achieved something – Joshua's voice
had been heard. And there was further satisfaction to
come.

Back at Levitstown, we found that John had prepared

a meal for us, a wholesome meal that satisfied our hunger, and that he had put in twenty drills of potatoes.

'Late in but good growers,' he laughed. 'They'll catch up.'

After our meal, we discussed the day's events and such was Joshua's enthusiasm that he convinced us that each of us could and would do what he had done.

That night, as we were drifting off to sleep, Abigail spoke to me.

'Can you see how he is, how he is to me?'

'I can,' I told her.

On the third Sunday of April, we travelled to Athy. Joshua had decided to bring his message to the doors of the Meeting House there and so we assembled in Meeting Lane at half-past ten in the morning. As the first Friends appeared in the narrow street he began preaching.

While he spoke we distributed our leaflets.

His preaching that morning was as I'd never heard it before.

'You are the outcasts of society,' he shouted as each group approached the Meeting House door. 'You were entrusted with the gift of Friendship and you rejected it. In your lives and behaviour you flew in the face of the Lord. You claim to walk in one light but you live in another. You are doomed unless you recognize the true Light and live in it. "Woe unto you, scribes and Pharisees, hypocrites, for ye shut up the kingdom of heaven against men: for ye neither go in yourselves, neither suffer ye them that are entering to go in."'

There was thunder in the faces of those going in and one of the Elders, Matthew McAuley, challenged Joshua on his words.

'You dare to preach in the street when your own life is a festering sore. You have left a wife and taken up with another man's wife and then you dare to confront us.'

'I walk in the Light of the Lord. I am a White Friend. You are Black Friends, cast out and doomed to hell for the way you have abused the Light.'

For a moment I believed Matthew was going to strike Joshua but instead he stormed inside the Meeting House, slamming the door behind him.

When the last of the Athy Friends had gone in, Joshua led us after them but we found the door locked against us. By now, the noise and confusion had drawn a crowd and Joshua began preaching to them.

'Inside this whited sepulchre are people who claim to be Friends but they are nothing less than the doomed and the damned. Their lives contradict everything that they claim to be. The Lord has spoken and we have followed Him out of this pit of vipers. Read the words that have been given to us. You may be saved. Your souls are for saving but for those locked inside the doors of this Meeting House there is no hope. They are locked inside their own hypocrisy and sin.'

His voice was so loud that he must have been clearly heard within.

He continued with his preaching and we with our

distribution of pamphlets until the crowds parted and a sergeant and two constables appeared before us.

The sergeant laid a hand on Joshua's shoulder.

'You're causing a breach of the peace,' he said, his face inches from Joshua's.

'I'm speaking the truth in the name of the Lord,' Joshua replied.

'Be that as it may,' the sergeant said. 'You can go your way quietly or we can take you with us.'

'"Yea though I walk through the valley of the shadow of death, I will fear no evil,"' Joshua continued.

The sergeant sighed, recognizing what he faced.

'Will you desist from this breach of the peace?' he asked.

'I will speak the Word given by the Lord, I will expose the hypocrisy of those who claim to be Friends but are nothing of the kind.'

The sergeant stepped back and Joshua resumed his preaching. He had spoken no more than a sentence when the sergeant nodded and the two constables grabbed Joshua's arms and marched him down the lane, followed by the sergeant.

William Ackworth was first to react.

'Stay here,' he said. 'I'll follow them. You stay here.'

And so we did. The crowd that had gathered remained a few minutes but when nothing happened they, too, left. We stood about, unsure of what we should do and, as we did, the Meeting House door opened and the Athy Friends appeared, led by Matthew McAuley.

72

Immediately, Abigail confronted them, blocking the narrow gateway that led from the small front yard into the lane. Her face was flushed and her eyes were brighter than light.

'You can go home smugly and sit and eat your meal and think you have done a good day's work in praying but you have done nothing. You are self-satisfied. You think that by attacking Joshua or me that you have found a weakness but you have found nothing but the emptiness in your own lives. You've lost the passion for life. You have nothing left but death and extinction.'

What a sight that was. One woman, dressed in a plain white dress, her dark hair drawn back tightly from her face, her skin pale but flushed, facing Matthew McAuley, a big, broad-shouldered man. And behind him two dozen others, crushed between the gate and the doorway.

She held them there in silence for some moments and then she spoke again.

'Go home now and be satisfied that a good man has been arrested because of your unfaithfulness. Go home but you'll never have peace in your lives again because you know he speaks the truth. Joshua was right when he called you Black Friends and from this day you'll live with that knowledge.'

And then she stepped aside and allowed them to pass, eyeing each in turn, daring them to speak but none did.

Thursday, May 28th

*

This is what I wrote today, a dull, overcast not altogether warm day.

*

When the Athy friends had dispersed, we made our way to the police barracks, where we met William Ackworth. After several enquiries, we were told that Joshua would be released later in the afternoon. On hearing this we were well pleased and William suggested we go back home. He would stay and accompany Joshua back to Levitstown. Abigail insisted that she, too, remain and such was the strength of her will that none opposed her.

Early in the evening, Joshua, William and Abigail arrived at the house and we ate a celebratory supper, happy that we had stood by the faith we professed. When the meal was ended, Joshua spoke.

'While I sat in my cell today,' he said, 'the Lord opened to me concerning our Friendship. And He said: "Are ye able to drink of the cup that I shall drink of, and to be baptized with the baptism that I am baptized with?" The question put to Zebedee's wife and children is the one He put to me and puts to you. And I answered as they did. "I am," I said and I felt the Light shine even brighter on me and the sorrow lift from me and it was

as if there were no walls or bars in that cell. And I was truly free.'

And then he said: 'We, too, will be baptized in the name of the Lord.'

I looked about the table and the surprise was plainly to be seen. Only Abigail seemed at ease with the suggestion.

*

Surprise? It wasn't surprise, it was dismay. Hadn't we all been brought up as good Friends, in the knowledge that baptism was not a part of our beliefs and never had been? And now Joshua was urging it upon us. True, Abigail showed no surprise, but Joshua might have suggested we walk on water and she would have stepped happily from the bank of the deepest river.

*

We discussed the matter a great deal but Joshua was adamant that this was the message opened to him.

William Ackworth and James Stubb, in particular, were dubious about this step but Joshua would give nothing in the face of their arguments.

'Did not John baptize? Did not Jesus come to be baptized? Was there not baptism of water and the Holy Ghost? Read Mark, read Luke, read Acts. I will not go back and throw His words in the face of the Lord. Will you be like the Black Friends, picking and choosing what does and doesn't satisfy? If so, then live with them but

don't live here. This will not become a house divided against itself.'

There was anger in Joshua's eyes when he spoke and neither William nor James seemed willing to engage him further.

As he rose from the table, Joshua looked to each in turn.

'The Lord is my light, you must decide whether you walk in that light or in darkness. You cannot walk two roads.'

And so he left us, retiring to his room.

John Wickham went into the garden and busied himself there while the rest of us talked quietly, trying to come to terms with the choice that faced us. It was a significant decision for all of us, a step beyond anything we had done before. It is no lie to say it was a greater shock to us than what had happened in Athy. There we had found an energy to preserve ourselves against those without but, in this case, we were faced with our own customs and a belief imbued in Friends for two hundred and fifty years. And we were not to have much time in deciding. The following morning, as we ate breakfast, Joshua asked of us, one by one, whether we were willing to be baptized. None refused.

On the first day of May, the first day of the summer of 1899, Joshua led us to a place on the River Barrow, half a mile from our house. There, in a secluded spot, overhung by willows which reached in from a meadow already filled with wild flowers, auguring a beautiful season, we stood uneasily on the river bank. The sun shone down on us and the breeze coming up the river promised June. But even the heat of the sun and the warmth of the breeze could not dispel the anxiety we felt at the prospect of baptism.

I do not know whether you are Friends. If you are, you will realize how extreme this step was. If not, you will not know how radical we were and how afraid.

Joshua was first to step into the water, wading among the iris spears and easing out into the flow until the water lapped his chest. Then he stopped, cupped his hands together and lifted them above his head. For an instant he held them there. We waited, watching for his hands to open and the water to fall, anticipating a bolt from heaven that would strike him dead, waited for the river to close about him and the current to carry him away. And then he spoke.

'"I baptize you with water unto repentance but He that cometh after me will baptize you with the Holy Ghost and with fire,"' he paraphrased John the Baptist and his hands opened and the water fell over his hair, streaming down his face and beard. He hesitated a moment before signalling John Wickham to go in.

John waded out until he was close to Joshua and then the act was repeated. William was next and then James Stubb and George Carr and me. Abigail was last of us all. In each case we waded out to where Joshua stood and he poured the water over our heads and repeated the words. When all had been baptized, we walked back to the house and changed into dry clothes.

*

But that isn't the all of it. There was more. Much more. The coldness of the water about my legs and body as I shuffled out from the warm, dry bank. My feet sucked into the slime of mud before it gave way to the colder, gravelly belly of the river bed. And the water rising, rising, the flow much faster than I expected. My mind on the evenings I sat in the boat on Ballitore pond when the water was still as stone about us. And then Joshua's hand, steady on my shoulder, the smile on his face, the water cupped above me, the words, the trickle over my hair and down my face, another steadying hand as I turned and made my way back to the bank where William leaned down to help me out of the water. And standing on the bank, the sun tepid now, my dress slapped against my skin. Watching Abigail make her way through the water, Joshua's smile again, his hands above her, the words and the way the water trickled down her face and onto her dress. As she turned and came back, pushing the water from her, her dress nuzzled the shape of her body and I felt as I had never done before. I wanted to step back into the water, to take her in my arms, to be the children she'd lost, to be the lover she'd dreamed, to be her comfort. It was all I could do to keep from rushing to her but I satisfied myself with reaching

78

down, with William, and helping her from the water. To touch her hand and feel the warmth under her arm when we lifted her from the sucking mud was adequate for then. But not enough.

Monday, June 1st

*

I took a few days for myself, after last week's efforts, and cycled, again, to Ballitore, up to the burial ground. I spent a pleasant hour there on Friday. It was an overcast morning but in the afternoon the sun came out and I sat by my parents' grave and considered the serenity and seclusion of sleep in that walled garden where snowdrops usher in the year and daffodils, wild anemones and bluebells, cowslips and primroses clutter the spring grasses. Where the leaves of the great trees and the bulk of the four stone walls keep out the excesses of summer heat and winter wind. Where the holly celebrates the Christmas time. I came away content with that because death is still almost an idyll and my body needs reminding now and then that it has all but grounded itself. There's no harm in that. I don't dither in the shadow of the valley but neither do I ignore it. I've neither set out to avoid the subject nor to bring it up at every hand's turn. If I allow myself, I can forget it for days on end and I don't like that. I don't relish the thought of my demise creeping in unnoticed. Come it will, as come it must, but I will know how close it is and when it comes it comes at my invitation and not like a thief in the night.

Mind you, through all of this, Dr Fullard calls twice a week and there's little chance of my forgetfulness running beyond the third day.

When he called, on Saturday morning, I told him this. He was appalled and flustered and I shouldn't be surprised if he doesn't come at all this week. He told me he thought I was a very ordered person in my approach to life.

'All my young life,' I told him, 'I fought against being dull and then, when I was forced to make my living from the dreary employment of housekeeping, I made some sense of it by the imposition of order. Order isn't stimulation but it saw me through.'

Poor man! He's confused, embarrassed, maybe even frightened by me.

I saw him off on Saturday with a request that he not play his uilleann pipes at my funeral. His response was to define an Irish gentleman as one who can play the uilleann pipes but doesn't. Touché!

Tuesday, June 2nd

*

Yesterday, I made several attempts to continue with my story but I couldn't find the words to commit the next section to paper so, instead, I wrote, again, to Friends in Dublin, enquiring whether there was any word of Lydia and Myfanwy. I intimated, without being specific, that I needed to contact them soon as time was not on my side.

*

Two days after our baptism, Joshua and your mother returned to the spot at the river and, such was their attachment, he anointed her again.

*

I followed them that morning. I saw them slipping out of the yard and crossing the road and climbing through the gap in the opposite ditch. I gave them no more than a minute start and then I followed, skirting along the opposite side of the ditch, keeping them in sight but never coming close enough to catch their conversation. I suspected that they were going to the river and I was right. They returned to the spot where we'd been baptized.

I don't know what I expected but as I sat on the slight

incline in the field behind the willows they undressed on the bank and then stepped into the water, wading hand in hand into the flow. When they were waist deep they stopped and Abigail stood with her back to me, her hair loose over her sallow shoulders, a rainbow of light and water coming off the arc of her neck.

And then Joshua began to speak and it was a time before I recognized the words.

' "Thy cheeks are comely with rows of jewels, thy neck with chains of gold. Behold, thou art fair, my love; behold, thou art fair; thou hast doves' eyes. As the lily among thorns, so is my love among the daughters." '

Words from the Song of Songs.

I sat, enthralled by what I was seeing, absorbed by what was happening. And then Abigail's voice, soft, barely discernible.

' "My beloved spake, and said unto me, Rise up, my love, my fair one, and come away. For, lo, the winter is past, the rain is over and gone; the flowers appear on the earth; the time of the singing of birds is come." '

When Joshua spoke his voice was clear, the words spoken with authority and not without feeling, but when Abigail spoke, it was obvious that she was searching for the words, straining to remember them, and so they came more haltingly and were all the lovelier for it.

How beautiful, I thought, and how apt. When she spoke those words, she meant them, they were hers and my heart went out to her. I wanted, more than ever, to be the one to comfort her. I wanted to be the lover of whom she spoke. In that moment, hearing those words, seeing her there in the sunlit river, I coveted her. And when she turned and waded back to the bank, when she stepped out of the water and stood naked before me, the river dripping from her, the sun pinning her body here and here and here, she was radiant and I ached to touch her, to trace the cold flow of water down her belly, down her thigh. I wanted to dam the drift of water from her shoulders with my mouth. I wanted to remove my own dress, to go down to the river, to embrace her. But I couldn't. I was frozen by her beauty and my fear.

All that afternoon, whenever I saw Abigail about the house, I wanted to tell her that I'd seen her at the river, not to embarrass or coerce her, but simply to share the excitement that burned in me. But, of course, I didn't. I was nineteen, I had no way of expressing that kind of feeling, and no way of knowing whether its expression was even possible. And that night, when Abigail got into bed, I lay listening to her breathing, waiting until I was sure she was asleep. Then I whispered my favourite lines from the Song of Songs into her sleeping ear.

'By night on my bed I sought him whom my soul loveth: I sought him, but I found him not.'

And then I whispered them again but changing them.

'By night on my bed I sought her whom my soul loveth: I sought her, but I found her not.'

I repeated the words over and over, hoping they might lodge somewhere in her head, that miraculously she might wake to the knowledge of my infatuation with her.

I've never dared write any of this before and I wonder if I've been unfair to myself in that?

*

On the Friday of that week, two men arrived at the house in Levitstown. I was the one who answered their knock and when they asked to see Joshua I took them into the kitchen and called him from his room.

When he saw them, he asked me to step outside awhile as he needed to speak to them in private.

I was happy to be released into the air and went down the garden, where I found John Wickham and two other local men, lying in the grass, taking the sun, their hands joined behind their heads, eyes closed to the blue sky, talking slowly about the merits of Kerr's Pinks and British Queens and Aran Banners. Their relaxed appearance reminded me of elderly men of my acquaintance in Ballitore, men who lay on the grassy banks on summer evenings, their hands behind their heads, in earnest talk of country matters.

John Wickham introduced me to the men, old men like himself, but their names are gone from me. I remained with them above an hour until I heard the visitors leave.

Then I returned to the house.

Joshua had retired to his room but Abigail, who had obviously been party to the conversation, told me what had fallen out.

The pair who called were Sarah Fayle's brothers, brothers-in-law to Joshua, and they had come to warn him of their unhappiness with our situation. They saw no reason, they said, why Sarah's business, which was part of a larger concern within her family, should subsidize the White Quakers. They pointed to the pamphlet printing, the renting of the house in Mountmellick and, now, the purchase of our house in Levitstown. All of these had been paid for by Sarah but the knowledge of her generosity had been kept from them until that week. On discovering it, they had urged her to sell the house and regain what money she could but she refused this and so they had come to talk to Joshua.

Their tone, Abigail said, had been unpleasant and they had left Joshua in no doubt about their intention to seek the support of the law in their attempt to repossess the property.

When he branded them Black Friends they left in a fury.

Thursday, June 4th

*

Yesterday, when I got back from shopping, I found a letter had come for me, from Friends in Dublin. It began with a fulsome apology for the delay in responding to my enquiry about Lydia and Myfanwy Beale. It transpires that research is continuing but it is known that neither woman is still a member of the Society of Friends in Ireland. The last, recorded, attendance of either woman at Meeting was over forty-five years ago. However, my correspondent tells me she is pursuing one or two other lines of enquiry and will be in touch as soon as she discovers anything. Of course I was disappointed, imagining there might be immediate news of the whereabouts of one or other of the sisters. But all is not lost.

*

Our next visit to Carlow, preaching and distributing pamphlets, came midway through that April. On this occasion, William Ackworth spoke first, sticking closely to the text of Psalm 23. When he had finished, Joshua took up the theme and captivated his audience, which until then had been restless, with talk of the life the White Friends offered – lying down in green pastures and walking by still waters. The picture he created was one of peace, accord, love and beauty and there was much truth in this for, despite the external pressures on Joshua, the house at Levitstown was a peaceful, prosperous and beautiful one. John Wickham was making of the garden a place of order and loveliness which promised even greater beauty with the arrival of summer. So, when Joshua spoke and people listened and were absorbed, I felt proud to be a part of the White Friendship. We all did. Listening to him speak and moving among the

*market-goers, distributing our pamphlets, the white garb
became an emblem of which to be proud.*

*

When Joshua talked of quiet waters, I caught Abigail's
eye and we exchanged smiles. I hoped mine told her
something of what I knew but I doubted it.

*

*Powerful and all as was Joshua's delivery, none of us
was ready for what happened next. At the end of the
afternoon, as we were preparing to leave for home, we
were approached by two young women who, it tran-
spired, were Friends living in Carlow. They introduced
themselves as sisters, Mary and Ann Fox, and expressed
an interest in joining the White Friendship.*

*Joshua spent a great deal of time in conversation with
them, giving them detailed directions on how to find the
house at Levitstown, while we stood about wishing he
would bring the conversation to a conclusion and allow
us to get home to our evening meal.*

*The sisters left us with the promise that we would see
them soon but, later that night, when Joshua had retired,
we discussed the matter and none showed any faith in
the promise.*

*James Stubb claimed to know their parents and
vouched that they would never allow their daughters to
step outside the fold.*

'And risk having them shut out? When James Fox gets

wind of the word of what his daughters are about, they'll be packed away.'

But, as in so many things, James Stubb was wrong.

The following Saturday Mary and Ann Fox arrived at our door, carrying two bags, and asking to be taken in as members of our Friendship. Despite our surprise, Abigail and I were not slow in reminding James of his words. His only reply was that we would see how long the sisters lasted before their father came in search of them.

And come he did, the following week, with the rest of their baggage and with his blessing for their membership. Abigail and I could not contain our amusement at James Stubb's discomfiture.

The Fox sisters became a part of our community that week. George Carr moved into the room shared by James and John while the sisters took up residence in what had been his room. At the end of that week, on a foggy morning, we gathered on the banks of the Barrow while Mary and Ann Fox were baptized into the White Friends.

I should say here that never a day passed that your names were not on your mother's tongue. And I must add that the arrival of the Fox sisters seemed to act as a great agitation to her spirit and a reminder that there were two other sisters for whose company she pined.

In the week following this, a letter came from your father and, as I write, I have before me the text of that missive.

Abigail Meredith:

The offspring of your onetime marriage, Lydia and Myfanwy Beale, are no longer resident at Rosenallis. As you have made no effort to contact your children there is no purpose in your knowing where they now reside. At their tender age they know nothing of your desertion, save that you are dead. And so you are, morally and spiritually. You await only your physical extinction, which cannot be long in following.

Robert Beale

This was a barbarous letter. Abigail had made many efforts to contact her family and, through them, to enquire of your well-being, but no response had been forthcoming from any source. Your father and your grandfather had closed her out and denied her even the courtesy of a response to her several enquiries. And then, to rub salt into her open wounds, this communication came after all her letters had been ignored, a savage twist which appalled all of us.

William Ackworth immediately requested permission to travel to Rosenallis and I was delegated to accompany him.

We made that journey on a day late in April, a day that was freshened by a warm breeze from the west that gave us comfort as we travelled the early miles from Levitstown. The trees, heavy in leaf, bent above our horse's head and billowed and twisted as the day grew deeper and the sun shrivelled the shadows about us.

We stopped at midday to eat the food we carried.

Sitting on the roadside in the shelter of an elm we discussed the events that were unfolding in your mother's life and William told me of his concern for her. And his concern was real. I can only assure you from this distance that William Ackworth and John Wickham and George Carr were genuine and generous people who were deeply troubled about your mother and about you. They recognized the attachment that exists between a mother and her children, the need that never ends and the dearth that is created by absence. They were honourable, kind and considerate people and they would have done anything to see you reunited with your mother.

We reached Rosenallis late that evening and went immediately to your father's shop. I had hopes, as we entered, that we might find him and you within but instead we were greeted by a young woman who told us that he had sold the shop and house and had left the village. When we enquired of your whereabouts she told us it was none of our business and added, for good measure, as she closed the door behind us, that no Friend would deal with 'sorcerers' such as us.

We travelled on to Mountmellich that night and requested an interview with Abigail's father. He came and stood on the steps of his house and denied any knowledge of a daughter.

At this, William became extremely angry.

'You have not turned out your daughter,' he said bitterly. 'You have no daughter because you never deserved

her. What father would turn his back on a child in pain? Your child is drowning and you're walking away from the river bank.'

With that he turned his back on your grandfather.

I stayed to make one last appeal to your grandfather but he did not respond and so I left and followed William to the cart and we went our way.

William refused to seek lodgings in Mountmellick and we journeyed an hour through the darkness before we found a place for the night.

Travelling back to Levitstown the following day, we tried to devise a way in which to ease your mother's disappointment but we could find none.

As we turned the cart into the yard, she came running from the house and we had no need to speak, for whatever hope she had gathered in her heart was shattered by the failure she plainly read in our faces.

The days that followed were alarming. Abigail took to walking alone through the fields about the house. We, in turn, followed her at a distance, such was our concern for her well-being. The weather had settled into a late spring of heat and light but we were hardly aware of it. The melancholy which clouded Abigail's life threw a pall over all of us. We went about our work but were ever conscious of your mother's despondency. We recognized the possibility that she would do herself an injury and it was a very real danger. On the few occasions when she spoke, her words were a threat to herself. There is no easier way of saying it.

Joshua's response to what had been done was one of anger. He travelled to Carlow the following Sunday, accompanied by James and William, and he berated the Friends there for their deceit. Somehow, he managed to get into the Meeting for worship and he refused to be silent or to leave when requested to do so.

He accused the Carlow Friends of being in league with those who had stolen you away from your mother.

William told me afterwards that Joshua stood at the front of the Meeting room and read from Matthew.

'In Rama there was a voice heard, lamentation and weeping, and great mourning, Rachel weeping for her children, and would not be comforted because they are not.'

He refused to be silenced and, in the end, the Carlow Friends were forced to abandon their Meeting. He followed them into the street, labelling each a Black Friend and warning them that those who came between a mother and her children, those who refused to act when faced with this separation, those who associated in any way with the people who had taken you, would be cast into darkness for evermore.

He strode through the streets of Carlow, stopping at the doors of Friends' houses and bellowing: 'Those who are not for the Lord are against Him. And woe to them for they are lost.'

And, while Joshua pursued the Carlow Friends, hounding them to their homes and putting them in fear of appearing in public, I followed Abigail through the meadows of Levitstown, close enough for her to know that I was there if she wished to talk to me but not making any conversation with her.

She drifted like a shadow through the long grass, her white dress billowing about her thin body, her dark hair taut about her pinched and frosted face.

The light had gone from her eyes, the glisten from her skin. She might have fallen down dead in the fields and we would not have been surprised. There was no life or ease about her any more, she who had always smiled a smile that would gladden our hearts had no expression at all. It was frightening to see the change that had been wrought in her life by one letter. The hope that was well hidden was also well rooted in her heart and that letter had all but severed its roots, leaving her with nothing. Let no one ever tell you that your mother lost you lightly. If she had, she would not have suffered as she did. The truth is she never lost you, never let you go from her heart or soul. She carried you with her in everything she did. Those who denied that love denied you the greatest gift.

*

This evening, as dusk drew on, I sat in my bedroom and watched the crows wheeling in above the Dominican church, flapping up the course of the Barrow and settling in the trees around the square. I counted fifty-seven and then I was too tired to count any more.

Friday, June 5th

*

A slight inconvenience but I woke this morning to find my right hand swollen and stiff. Too much writing yesterday.

I visited Dr Fullard in his surgery this afternoon. I was out walking and called on a whim. He wasn't particularly busy and we chatted a while. He walked me to the door and as we parted he said: 'Doctors get things wrong, too, you know. Six months could be ten years.'

I asked if he was trying to give me hope when there was no reason for hope.

'No,' he said. 'It's just that I've been thinking about things and we do get it wrong, all of us, even the specialists. We have no knowledge of the heart or the soul.'

I laughed and told him I was sure the cardiac specialists would disagree.

'You know what I mean,' he said.

I nodded.

'Just remember that, then.'

I told him he was preaching to a believer.

I think he was pleased with that.

When I reached his gateway I turned and he was still standing at the surgery door.

'Are you a passionate man, Dr Fullard?' I asked.

'Why?'

'I'm testing you.'

And I left him with that thought and walked back down past the railway gates, past Mount Offaly house, back here.

And so I am testing him. If I reach a point where I have told the story for Lydia and Myfanwy and if, by then, I can do no more, I may need someone to ensure the truth gets to them.

Saturday, June 6th

*

Today was so beautiful with the kind of sky a friend once described as a Portuguese sky, a blue so deep it was only kept afloat by the wisps of cloud that crossed it now and then.

I walked the Barrow track, beyond Ardreigh lock and found a place to sit, a place well shaded. I was no more than three miles from the spot where we'd been baptized. A terrible sadness came over me. No, maybe not a sadness, a craving for the carnal, a craving for Abigail, the kind of longing that was so much a part of my life when we lived in Levitstown. A craving that's come back periodically over the years. There were times, in England, when I was in my thirties and forties and fifties, in the years before and after the Great War, when I'd exist for weeks in a state of semi-consciousness, haunted by Abigail. Not by memory but by need, by this appalling frustration, necessity faced with despondency. I wanted her, then, even more than I'd wanted her when she was alive and her absence only barbed my longing. For years that longing was a constant, unpredictable visitor but it had disappeared in the last two decades. And today it was back again. I lay in the long grass by the river and longed for Abigail's body. Longed to unbraid her hair, to slip her dress from her shoulders. I sank into that craving and there was nothing I could do until it passed of its own accord.

How strange to be faced with death and to find lust bustling about its murky doorway. And how cheering! I notice a growing fondness for the exclamation mark. Why not!!!!!!!

Monday, June 8th

*

Joshua did endeavour to lift your mother's spirits. He was more than attentive to her in those days and was at pains to ensure our presence in his absence. We prayed at that time more than we had ever prayed before. We would gather each night in the kitchen and Joshua would lead our invocation, speaking with great conviction, promising that God would not deny us strength, reminding us of the trials the first disciples went through.

He returned, constantly, to Romans: 'We glory in tribulations.'

I cannot say these words were of great comfort to your mother but they seemed to keep us together and we, in turn, kept her from despondency. And you were in our prayers, too. Your welfare was our concern, your absence our distress. Our determination to bring your mother from her misery was fortified by our care for your well-being.

*

I found myself, at this time, spending most of my days with Abigail. When I wasn't with her I was following her and when Joshua was in her company I made it my business not to be far away. The arrival of the Fox sisters had taken much of the pressure of housework off my shoulders and, whenever I could, I followed Joshua and Abigail. I realize few people will understand this, seeing it as a callous invasion of their privacy, but I didn't and don't see it in that light.

I was besotted with Abigail. I shared her bed, I wanted her, I craved her touch and each time I put my arm about her, to comfort her, to hold her when she cried, it was all I could do to keep myself from kissing her.

The most pleasant times of those days were the times when I sat in the garden at the back of our room, Abigail sitting at my feet, trying to brush the vitality back into her hair, braiding the long dark strands, telling her how beautiful she was, craving some response, some sign of happiness returning. But there was none. I promised her that we'd find Lydia and Myfanwy, that we'd get them back for her, that they were not lost, but when she responded at all it was to dismiss my optimism.

The last day of that month, April 1899, was a Sunday, and instead of travelling to Carlow, Joshua took Abigail with him, down to the river bank. I followed them. They stood, face to face, under the trees at the spot where we'd been baptized. His hands were on her shoulders and he held her as a father might hold a child, willing the energy and protection that he could offer to travel from his body into hers and yet when he spoke he talked to her, not as a child, but as an equal. His tone was neither hectoring nor pitying.

'You are the mother of the generations,' he said. 'Just as I am the messenger of the Lord. As the Lord has spoken to me so He has made demands of you. You have not lost your children, you have become the mother of this generation and generations to come. You will recover your children and number them with the other children at your knee. The Lord has sent this as a test, as He sent a test to Abraham. You will not be found wanting. In spite of everything, nothing will be lost to you because you are the one He has chosen.'

It appeared to me that little or nothing would come of this encounter but I was wrong. I can't for whatever reason come to tell Lydia and Myfanwy of that incident.

There was an intimacy about it, or at least my memory lends it an intimacy, that will not be shared.

Anyway, it isn't essential to what followed.

*

On the evening of the last day of April of that year, we gathered in the kitchen of the house in Levitstown, as we did every evening, for our meal. It was eaten mostly in silence, as all our meals were at that time, for we could not rid ourselves of the gloom that had come with your father's letter.

When we had eaten, Joshua rose from his chair and spoke very quietly, his words punctuated by silences.

'The Lord said to Abraham: "Take now thy son, thine only son Isaac, whom thou lovest and get thee into the land of Moriah and offer him there for a burnt offering upon one of the mountains which I will tell thee of."

'And Abraham did as the Lord bade him do. He went in sorrow but he went. He had been asked to sacrifice his child, his only child, yet he trusted in the will of the Lord. He brought his son to be sacrificed, to be given up. In spite of everything. In spite of the terror within. He trusted in the Lord. And the Lord repaid his trust. Abraham was chosen because he was worthy of the choice.

'Abigail has been chosen, too. Chosen to suffer the pain of loss, to lose her children. But they are not lost. The Lord has made her the mother of the generations. She is a chosen one.'

He paused here for a long time and then turned to Abigail and said: 'You have not lost, you have gained the love of the Lord and the motherhood of the generations who will look to you for succour and comfort. Rejoice in the love of God.'

And she did. Her face seemed, suddenly, miraculously to shine and she rose from her chair and spoke.

'Joshua has told me the Lord blesses me and I believe him because his words are the words of the Lord. Lydia and Myfanwy are mine and they will be with me again. I have been journeying like Abraham, and Joshua has come like the angel to tell me my children are saved. I will have them again at my knee.'

*

Her words were an echo of Joshua's but such was my delight at seeing this transformation I didn't begrudge him or her the happiness that was obvious to us all, a happiness we shared. It was only later that I saw the gap between what Joshua said and what Abigail heard.

*

I do not wish you to think Abigail stepped out of one light and into another, that her sorrow fell from her like leaves. Her sorrow was constant. Only the rest of her life varied, stretching and shrinking, but always with anguish at its core.

Monday, June 15th

*

I've never known such pain or such perseverance of pain as I've known in the past week. Last Tuesday afternoon I cycled out towards Castledermot. I intended getting to Kilkea, spending an hour there and then returning. But I knew before I was halfway there that something was wrong. I rested a long time but the feeling of nausea and the pain that had begun so gradually would not go away. Eventually, I swallowed my pride and wheeled my bike to the nearest house. I was fortunate that they had a telephone. They called Dr Fullard and he came, immediately, and collected me and drove me directly to his surgery and gave me an injection. Then he took me home and insisted on waiting until I was safely in bed. Mrs Murphy stayed with me. Dr F. called back that evening but the pain was worse by then, so he gave me another injection. Sometime the following morning, three or four, I asked Mrs Murphy to send for him again. I could barely endure the pain. It was torment. Another injection. Then I slept. Maybe for twelve hours. When I woke I was still in agony. I wanted to die, I don't deny it. One thing I know, now, if there's pain, real pain, death is welcome.

I think Dr F. thought I was dying, too. He made no attempt to have me hospitalized. I believe he thought it too late for that. He called twice and three times a day. Each time I woke, Mrs or Mr Murphy were there. I never woke alone. What comfort in that. I'm blessed, twice blessed in the Murphys and in Dr Fullard.

Each time I fell asleep, I hoped for relief and each time I woke to endless pain. Not that I really woke, I was constantly drugged but the medicine was never enough to appease the pain. I can only make the clichéd notes now – it ate me, burned me, took my breath away, left me without the will to live or the capacity to die. My little energy went into willing myself away but my resolution was nothing. Fortitude is so far short of what you need. I can't explain this. I was terrified by the depth and continuance of my pain and I was appalled by my inability to do anything. You can't shake life off. You want to but you can't.

It was only yesterday that I began to consider anything other than the relief that death would bring.

Wednesday, June 17th

*

I woke this morning with the date fixed in my head. This is the date of Lydia's birthday. June 17th and October 7th. Lydia and Myfanwy. Only after I'd clarified that in my head was I aware of the absence of pain. Yesterday less pain than before. Today no pain at all. I waited. I talked to Dr F. about it. And to Mrs Murphy.

'I suppose you'll tell me next that you miss it,' she said when I told her I expected its return.

Saturday, June 20th

*

Today I got up. Sat in the back yard. The sun shone. Four days without pain. Dr F. called only once. I begin to think I've staved it off. For now.

Sunday, June 21st

*

Summer solstice. A hot day. A long day. I enjoyed the warmth and the brightness. I enjoyed the day. That's enough. 'Take therefore no thought for the morrow, for the morrow shall take thought for the things of itself.'

Matthew something or other. All is not forgotten!

Monday, June 29th

*

A beautiful week gone by. Strength. Health. If health is not too grand a word for the absence of pain. I'm out and about again. To be out and about is such a marvellous thing. Out and about. Alive. Moving. The instability of life is a positive thing. Stability is being nailed to the same bed, the same chair, the same room. I'm unstable again, I wander the town and just because I can. I go in and out of shops. I did today. I took my time over things. I gathered an enormous bunch of sweet-pea that was growing wild down the Crib Road. Being alive is being unstable. Being dead is being stable for ever. I'm alive. I don't dare think of staying alive because that's to hope for too much but each fresh warning, each knock on the door, makes the time in between all the sweeter.

Tuesday, June 30th

*

I've just reread what I wrote yesterday. It seems like poppycock. As though. As though what? As though. Enough to say as though. I know.

Will this wild, pointless optimism begin to haunt me like another kind of pain?

Friday, July 3rd

*

I think I've regained my equilibrium. Sanity. Some of the pain has returned in the past few days. Gnawing rather than wrenching. It's as though I needed it, to bring me back to reality.

Tonight, sitting in my bedroom, the window open, heat outside and in, a slice of moon in the sky, some kind of flying beetle crash-landed on the window sill. It was stunned by the hardness of its landing, walked about a moment or two, uncertain, then folded its wings very neatly, very slowly and died. No, no, not a message or a warning, nothing so conceited. Just that, just what it was. That's all there is. No pretension or anything like that. Just us folding our little wings here and there and trying to be of some consequence. I must return to my attempt at consequence. I'd very much like to see it through.

Saturday, July 4th

*

Last night I dreamt but the dreams were more memories, dredged up from that part of the brain that holds these things, waiting for a time and place where they're important.

In the first part of the dream, I was standing at the door of the house in Levitstown. It was summer and it was raining. I was looking out from the doorway, across the wet yard, and Abigail turned in at the gate, coming off the roadway, alone. Her hair hung down each side of her face. Her dress was sodden but she was smiling and her smile was enchanting.

Later in the dream, or in another dream, Abigail was sitting on a gate at the side of the same roadway. I knew the gate, it was two fields down from the house, on the Carlow side. Her legs were dangling just above the ground, her feet were bare and she swung them back and forth between the wooden bars and, again, she was smiling.

What I found in the dreams were lost memories but I've found them and they urge me on. So, today, I begin again.

*

I have memories of your mother from that time, the time when she began to recover her health and hope. Memories of her in the rain, smiling in spite of the rain. Memories of her about the garden, working with John Wickham and me, weeding and cleaning and clearing. Memories of her in the evening, sitting on a field gate, swinging her legs carelessly, though she was not careless.

The first week of May that year turned extremely hot and clear. At the end of the week, Joshua announced that he was going to spend four days away from us, in expectation of further openings. And so, on Monday the eighth of May, he took his leave of us and went to live in the open countryside.

I thought his absence might provoke a further bout of depression in your mother but it was not so. She accepted it as she accepted most things and got on with her life.

Indeed, she and I spent much of that week in high spirits, trying to avoid the Fox sisters, who had turned the pleasures of making a home into the tedium of regimentation. One of our delights was to put the knives and forks and spoons willy-nilly into the drawers of the press and then to watch Mary and Ann Fox sort them out again, each to its own section of the drawer. Such were our innocent seditions.

*

There were other, less childish pleasures! We'd talk late into the night about the Fox sisters. We thought very little of them and they had no time for our skittishness. Mary was twenty-four, a year older than Abigail, and Ann was three years younger than her sister. Ann was extremely beautiful, with fair hair that set off her dark skin. Mary, on the other hand, walked with a severe limp and her face, though handsome, was stamped by a large purple birthmark. Her hair was lank and her eyes were dull, it seemed to us. In spite of the contrast in their physical appearance, they shared the same dour manner. At that time, we despised them.

*

Joshua returned to us on the evening of the following Friday, the twelfth day of May. The weather was still hot and dry. We had spent every evening of that week drawing water to irrigate the vegetables and fruit in the garden. Already the flowers were in full flush.

We were working in the garden that evening, too, dizzily giggling as we staggered under the weight of the buckets and the greater weight of the baleful stares of James Stubb and the Fox sisters. In the midst of all this, Joshua walked through the gateway, his skin dark and shining from his days in the sun. At the sight, all work was forgotten. We gathered about him in the yard, welcoming him, waiting on his words but there were none. He smiled at each of us but the warmest smile was reserved for Abigail.

The Fox sisters hurried to prepare a meal for Joshua, as I myself had done many times. While he ate, we con-

tinued our work in the garden and it was only when darkness threatened that we drifted inside.

I expected Joshua to retire, as he often did when he returned from these excursions, but instead he sat with us a long time. When he did speak his tone was uncertain.

'The Lord directed me first and last to the Book of Deuteronomy. Chapter five, verse thirty-three. "Ye shall walk in all the ways which the Lord your God hath commanded you." The Lord told me this and then He opened to me that I should cut all binds to those who are not of our belief. Abigail has done this. All of you have left your families to be White Friends. Now the Lord has opened to me that I must do the same. He has told me that I should divorce myself from all that was, from my family and money and wife.'

The importance, the absolute tumult of what he was proposing did not register with us then. It was only when he continued that we saw the unimaginable breadth of what he was suggesting and even then we dared not believe our own ears.

'The Lord opened to me,' he continued, 'not once or twice but thrice and each time His words were the same.

'We must walk all the ways He directs us, those we understand and those we do not. Our faith depends on our willingness to walk in the Light, even when we do not understand where the Light may lead us. And so I am walking where the Lord directs. He has told me to *put my wealth, my family and my wife away from me and I will do as the Lord commands. He has told me to take Abigail as my wife and I will do as the Lord commands.'*

I cannot describe the hush which followed this pronouncement. Even the late birds seemed to have been silenced by it.

Finally, George Carr spoke.

'And this is the word of the Lord?'

'This is what the Lord has opened to me, not once or twice but thrice.'

'It will make Abigail's life and your life hard.'

'I cannot see it,' James Stubb interjected. 'I cannot see the hand of the Lord in this. It will make life impossible for us all. It will bring the weight of the world onto our heads. Have you thought of this? What this will do? This flies in the face of . . . of . . . of God, of everything.'

The sentences came out in a tumble, one word falling over the next.

'I will do as the Lord asks,' Joshua said.

'And what of Abigail?' William Ackworth enquired. 'Has anyone considered her position?'

'I will do as the Lord asks,' she repeated quietly and the strength and certainty in her voice were most impressive.

Nothing more was said that night and we all retired to our rooms soon afterwards.

*

Abigail and I talked all night, until the earliest light watered our window.

'How could I refuse this?' she asked me. 'This is what I want, who I want.'

'Do you believe it's the will of God?'

She shrugged.

'I want him, Elizabeth, I want him to have me. When I think of him I think of his arms about me, I think of falling asleep and waking with his arm about me. I think of the smell of his skin.'

As she spoke, I thought of the irony of what she was saying. Of how this was what I longed for from her but I had never dared to say it and I wouldn't now.

Sunday, 5th July

*

The days which followed Joshua's announcement were tense ones. At every opportunity, the subject of his relationship with Abigail and the difficulties the other White Friends had with it were discussed. Each evening the subject came up during our meal and Joshua's response was always the same.

'The Lord has opened to me, am I to contradict the Lord? Are we only to accept what we find easy to accept?'

There was no response to this, short of questioning the validity of the opening.

Eventually, James Stubb did this and Joshua's reply was simple and to the point.

'If you accept the other openings, why can you not accept this?'

'Because it flies in the face of the word of God in His teachings.'

'These are His teachings,' Joshua replied coldly.

'In His teachings in the Testaments.'

'Why are you here, then?' Joshua asked. 'You were happy to be here when the teachings suited you, are you a fair-weather Friend?'

'You have no right to say this to me,' James Stubb retorted, his face reddening and his hands trembling. 'I have accepted everything you taught and never wavered from what you told us but I have doubts, grave doubts, about what you are proposing.'

Joshua said nothing.

'All of us have problems with what you are saying,' George Carr said. 'You cannot be surprised at that.'

Joshua looked about the table and his eyes rested on William Ackworth.

'And you, William,' he asked, 'do you have problems?'

'I do,' William said.

'Elizabeth?' he asked.

'I am concerned with what this may do, how others may view us.'

He nodded. 'But you, do you have problems?'

I shook my head.

'Abigail?' he continued.
'I will do as the Lord asks,' she replied.
'Ann?'
She shook her head.
'Mary?'
Again, a shake of the head.
'John?'
'No, I am content.'
'I cannot undo what the Lord has done or unsay what He has said,' Joshua continued. 'Only the Lord can do that. I will go away tonight, I will return in four days. I will leave myself open to His word. That is all I can do.'
And so he went.

*

When Joshua asked my opinion my mind was a riot. Of course, I doubted what he had been told. How could I not? I doubted everything that he said and did, as I had doubted everything my parents had brought me up to believe. And of course my mind was torn at the thought of Abigail leaving my room, our bed, and going to his and that I saw as an inevitability. I knew more of their doings than they imagined and I had more reason than most to doubt Joshua's motives but I could not coldly reject his proposal. If I did I'd be turning my back on Abigail, saying that I for one was not prepared to accept what I knew to be her greatest desire.

*

In Joshua's absence we talked and talked about the opening, if opening it had been. The discussion went about in hoops and circles always falling back to the two, divided, opinions.

If this was not the word of the Lord then how were we to know the previous openings were His either?

Or, if this was the word of the Lord, then how could it be explained in the light of the Bible?

And so the arguments continued.

James Stubb was adamant that Joshua was suffering delusions, that his time in the sun, without proper food or drink, was affecting his mind.

'And he'll return again, starved and droughted, and of a like frame,' he argued. 'Nothing will have changed in or out of his head.'

Ann Fox, rarely heard on religious matters before this time, was equally vocal in Joshua's support.

'Because you cannot accept this, you cannot allow the rest of us to accept it either. You are trying to bully us into agreeing with you. Go if you have to but don't try to pull the White Friends asunder when you do.'

Both William and George tried, quietly, to talk to Abigail but her answer, as always on this question, was: 'I will do as the Lord asks.'

Monday, 6th July

*

This morning a letter came from Friends in Dublin, apologizing, again, for the delay in responding to my enquiry but saying that a blank has been drawn.

As they told me in the first letter, there is no trace of Lydia or Myfanwy in any Meeting in Ireland and, now, I'm told they have not surfaced in any Meeting in England, either.

For a few moments I was tempted to abandon everything, to sit down and count the hours and minutes and seconds remaining, but as I allowed my mind to toy with the idea there was a knock on the door and I opened it to find Dr Fullard outside. He had been on call in the street and popped in to say hello.

'You look well,' he said.

'Not as well as I was ten minutes ago,' I told him.

'Oh?'

'A little disappointment,' I said.

I offered him some tea and we sat in the kitchen, chattering. And then he enquired, out of the blue, why I'd asked him if he was a passionate man.

'Strange you should ask,' I said. 'It has to do with the disappointment I had this morning.'

I told him about my undertaking, to find Lydia and Myfanwy, to tell them the story.

'I wondered whether, if I don't find them, if I don't have time, whether I might find someone who would undertake to deliver the account to them.'

'And it would have to be someone with a passion,' he laughed.

'Yes,' I said. 'And someone who won't be judge-mental.'

'Of what?' he asked. 'If I undertake to deliver this – if you need someone to deliver it – why should I want to know what's in it? That wouldn't be part of the agree-ment. You can trust me on that.'

'Are you saying you'll do it, if I need you to?'

'Yes, I am.'

'That's very generous,' I said. 'It may not come to that, of course. There may not be a trace of either of them.'

'Why don't we both do our piece,' Dr F. said. 'You finish what you're writing. Let me see if I can unearth anything on these people. Can you give me any infor-mation on them?'

I gave him the names, birthplace and dates and he undertook to do his best for me. And I'm sure he will. His enthusiasm was catching. I got back to work immediately.

*

In the days of Joshua's absence, there was a tension in the house at Levitstown. When the subject of the openings was not under discussion, it was on everyone's mind.

Only John Wickham seemed capable of stepping outside the controversy and getting on with his work. It was
to John that I turned in times when my own mind was
overrun with doubts. His closeness to nature, his oneness
with the soil, his love for his work, were in constant evi-
dence. No matter what the trouble, John was happy in
his garden and simply to be there with him spread that
happiness like a contagion.

He never sought out anyone but when one of us came
to him we could rely on his support and comfort. I know
Abigail spoke with him many times in that period,
too, and found the same comfort that I had done. His
philosophy was simple – judge not that you may not be
judged.

Other than John and Abigail, William Ackworth also
spoke with me a number of times and I was aware that
his heart and head lay in different directions. He had
followed Joshua Jacob faithfully and that faith would not
easily be shaken but he found this latest test extremely
difficult to deal with.

Those four days crept by, and as they ended the
anxiety rose within our little community. All that fourth
day and into the evening, we glanced continually at the
gateway, expecting at every moment the figure of Joshua.
Strange that all of us were working in and around the
yard that evening, dragging the simplest task beyond its
due, wanting to catch a glimpse of his face, expecting an
answer from that glimpse.

But we were to be disappointed. The afternoon and

evening passed and the Fox sisters went inside to prepare the evening meal.

That night Abigail and I lay awake, whispering and listening for Joshua's return. The thought crossed my mind that something might have happened to Joshua, that he might have fallen and injured himself, that he might have decided not to return, reconsidering his situation and deciding that flight was the better part of valour.

I didn't mention this but Abigail seemed to discern my thoughts and it was she who raised the question in order to dismiss it.

'He will come back, even now he's coming back,' she said resolutely.

'How can you know that?' I asked.

'I don't need to know it. I know him. That's all there is to know.'

There was no debating this opinion, I recognized that fact from her tone.

'And when he comes,' she continued, 'it will be to take me as his wife. It was ordained by God.'

'And by Joshua,' I added.

'And by me,' she returned.

I was silent then.

After a time, she asked: 'Why do you take what I say so personally?'

'Because I'm your friend, because I fret for you, because I never want to see you hurt again.'

'Nor shall I be, Elizabeth. You are my friend and always will be. Nothing will change that. Our friendship isn't going to end. It can only deepen. Believe me.'

'But you'll go to Joshua, you'll become his wife.'

'Yes. I love Joshua. And I love you. I love both of you. Just as I didn't stop loving Lydia and Myfanwy and never will, so I'll never stop loving you.'

*

But that isn't what she said. She said: 'I love Joshua. And I love you. I love both of you, but I can't be your wife, can I?' And she laughed. It was a gentle laugh but it cut me because more than anything I wanted to be the one who took her as a mistress, wife, whatever. I hardly understood what it was that I craved for us, needed for myself. All I knew was that I wanted to christen her with fragile, tender names. I longed to whisper words to her, call her darling, sweetheart, beloved, lover, love. But I didn't.

*

I was happy to know I held such a place in her heart, close to you, but I was unhappy about her commitment to Joshua for I felt it could only mean further pain for her. It was inevitable that she and Joshua would be attacked from within and without the White Friends. He might weather such a storm – indeed, I believed at that time, not knowing him as I was later to know him, that *he might thrive on it – but I knew your mother well enough to recognize that the brave face she displayed might easily be shattered, leaving her helpless and hopeless.*

We talked a little more that night and then we slept.

Sometime later I heard voices in the kitchen and I crept down to find Joshua and William seated at the table. Neither spoke when I entered and a few moments later Joshua rose from his seat, drained the mug of tea he was drinking and said: 'I bid you both goodnight.'

When he had retired, William said: 'There is to be no change. He will marry Abigail. All of us will suffer, one way or another.'

Then he rose from his chair.

'Now we should retire,' he said. ' "Take no thought for the morrow: for the morrow shall take thought for the things of itself. Sufficient unto the day is the evil thereof." '

'You believe it will come to that?'

'It has come already. Only sleep prevents the others from knowing it. Now you should sleep, too.'

He laid his hand on my shoulder and there was safe-keeping, sadness, confusion in that one gesture.

I felt for William Ackworth, felt for his desolation and the responsibility that he saw falling on himself but there was nothing I could do to comfort him.

I watched him to his room and I blew out the candles in the kitchen and inched my way through the darkness to our room.

*Your mother was asleep and I listened to her breathing
and hoped she would not be asked to shoulder more than
she could bear.*

*

I listened to her breathing and I knew I might never
share her bed again and I began to cry. My tears came,
great gulping, silent tears. I lay there while they slid
down my cheeks, onto the bolster beneath my head.
Only when they had ceased did I dare to do what I had
wanted to do for so long. I leaned across Abigail's sleeping body and whispered that I loved her, that I could
not believe in a life without her. I wanted to kiss her
but I didn't. Instead, I touched the curl of her hair, ran
my fingers along the rainbow of her neck and whispered,
again, to her sleeping form, that I loved her.

I'd love to tell Lydia and Myfanwy this. Perhaps, if
we meet, I'll find the courage.

Why is it, in the face of annihilation, that I can't bring
myself to tell them everything? Not for fear of what
they'd think of me but for fear it might reinforce whatever destructive notions their father may have planted
in their minds.

Tuesday, 7th July

*

I have to be patient. I woke this morning wondering whether Dr F. had made any progress in his search. In twenty-four hours? Hardly! Be patient, Elizabeth, continue the work and when that's done you can worry. Which is what I've done.

*

Given William's dire warning, I had expected a confrontation the following morning, when Joshua's decision became known. Sometimes reality disappoints our worst expectations and so it was in this case. By the time Joshua called us together, sometime before noon, all of us knew what he would say.

When it came, his statement was short. The Lord had not opened to him again. He had fasted and abstained, he had stayed awake night and day and when he slept it was in readiness for a dream opening but none came.

'The Lord spoke to me and said what He had to say. He has not spoken again. Why should He? If we cannot accept His word that is our quandary, not His.'

There followed a long silence, a silence that challenged the listeners. Finally, James Stubb rose from his seat near the open kitchen door. The light from the sun-drowned yard piled up behind him in the opening so that all we could see was a dark frame, without face or expression. From this dim form a voice came, as though from someone else, softly almost, certainly devoid of the harshness and acidity I expected.

'I cannot believe what you believe, Joshua. I did believe and, God knows, I wish to continue my belief for I can never go back to what I was, but neither can I go onward with you. You cannot put away a wife to take another. You have taken a wife and nothing will change that – not your openings or your words or anything.'

He paused for an instant and turned and, from where I sat, I was convinced the sunlight caught a tear on his face. This, I thought, is worse than confrontation, this sadness that pervades the place, that saps the life and happiness and hope and spirit out of all of us. And then I heard a voice and as it spoke I recognized it for my own.

'I have often disagreed with you, James Stubb,' I was saying, 'and I know you don't place me highly in your regard but I think it would be a great sadness if you were to leave us. Different as we are, all of us, we have endured much together and should continue in that endurance. I would like you to stay, in spite of all.'

He turned to face me and he smiled.

'Thank you, child, but I cannot.'

With that he backed away and stepped outside. I saw him pick a bag from the ground and make off across the yard. William rose from his chair and followed. Through the open doorway I could see them in conversation at the *gateway and then James shook William's hand and he was gone and we never saw him again.*

Friday, 10th July

*

I've spent the past three days in the fear of death, in terror, and all from so little, yet I can't shake the terror from me.

On Wednesday morning, I was shopping, buying bread from the bakery, when a man came in and fell into conversation with one of the assistants. They bantered awhile and she asked him how his business was.

'As good as ever. No shortage,' he laughed.

The assistant laughed, too.

'Aren't you the lucky man, the only undertaker in the town. We'll all fall under your spell.'

The man clapped his hands, melodramatically.

'I certainly hope so,' he said.

I felt, not a shiver, more a weakness, the energy draining from me and I knew nothing could replenish it. Not the sunshine in the street outside, not the return to my writing, not medicine. Nothing.

I tried to back away, to escape the sound of the man's voice, but the assistant was still wrapping the bread I had bought and the man was still joking and laughing at the other end of the counter. I was no longer aware of the words he was saying, merely of the tone of his voice. Each time he spoke, the sound of his voice sucked my energy further. I dared not look at him. I was petrified. Coarse fear had taken hold, has taken hold of me.

I took the parcel of bread when it came and shuffled from the shop into which I'd walked with a spring in my step. I found my legs would not obey me. Out of habit they moved but my feet never left the ground.

I stood on the footpath, waiting to cross Leinster Street, waiting to get back here, but first a bus and then several cars came from the direction of the station.

And while I waited for the last car to pass I saw a shadow fall in front of me and I heard the voice, the same voice, the voice I can't get out of my head.

'Can I give you a hand across?'

'No, no, no,' I said. Loudly, rudely, but I didn't care.

The car passed and I crossed as quickly as I could, making the opposite path, steadying myself with a hand against the hotel wall, edging my way around the corner at Dallon's shop, passing O'Brien's and the Town Hall, across Offaly Street and in here. Only then did I allow myself to be sick, to collapse in the echo of that voice. Later, when I slept, I dreamt I heard it and that, too, terrorized me.

The voice, the tone of voice, haunts me like a chord of death. No, that doesn't do justice to how it has ravaged me in three days. Sleeplessness, nightmares when I do sleep. And a fear of going out, a fear of hearing that voice again.

Yesterday was no better. I'd hardly slept on Wednesday night and when I did sleep, sometime about mid-morning yesterday, I fell into a deep slumber from which there seemed no escape. And I dreamed. In the dream, I knew I was in bed, I knew I was asleep but I knew, too, that the footsteps on the stairs were those of the undertaker, the nameless, faceless man. I have no recollection of his face. If I met him in the street I wouldn't know him, and that's even more frightening. I've no recollection of his features, no way of preparing myself. All I know, know too well and cannot escape, is the pitch of his voice.

There's nothing in what he said, nothing beyond the hackneyed, but that, too, is frightening. The casual way of his conversation, his words like the scatter-holes of nails in old floorboards, random but unavoidable.

Even that leads me back to yesterday's dream. Lying on my bed, the footsteps on the stairs and landing, the sense of his presence in the room. And then his going away again and returning, this time with a heavier step, with other steps, with the clattering of timber against the banisters. I knew it was my coffin on the stairs, on the landing, the sound of my coffin laid on the bedroom floor. And, in my dream, I felt myself lifted off my bed, felt the cold, crisp cloth of the coffin lining against the back of my legs. Smelt the fresh wood. Sensed the darkening of the gloom beyond my eyelids as the top was screwed into place. My senses were alert, primed even, but I couldn't speak. The smell of the closed box. The touch of the cheap cloth irritating my skin. And the sound of that voice. The resonance which, though muffled, was unmistakable. Through all this, through the real and imagined sleep, the voice was there. Prosaic, matter of fact, final.

And, after the dream, after the relief of waking, there were the other banal matters – sweating, vomiting, diarrhoea, the stone in my stomach any time I've thought of eating.

I'm frightened.

People think that because you live alone, because you've lived alone all your life, you must be brave. If only they knew. Aloneness is no protection against fear because fear is so ordinary. There's no protection.

I'm afraid. Afraid to sleep. Afraid to dream. Afraid to go out. Afraid of the warm day outside, resentful of the sunshine in my patch of yard, afraid of life and death. Cowardice makes me wince and flinch at every knock on the door.

This afternoon I began to calculate, again, the weeks and days and hours and minutes and seconds left to me but I left the calculation unfinished because I've no way of going on with anything. This is dread. This is a kind of madness.

I'm insane.

Tuesday, 14th July

*

I'm surprised to find myself writing again but I write in
spite of everything, not because of anything. Surprised
to have come through the weekend, surprised – despite
the weakness inside – how much torture my body and
brain can inflict and accept.

Thursday, 16th July

*

It's over a week now and still, whenever I have to answer
the door, to the delivery boy or the Murphys or Dr F.,
I expect to hear that voice. Its matter-of-factness.

Saturday, 18th July

*

Yesterday and, again, today I woke without the dryness
in my throat. The first signs of a return to something
close to normality. Saying that is probably tempting fate.

Sunday, 19th July

*

I look back over the past ten days, almost two precious weeks, and I know I've gone through a kind of collapse, breakdown I suppose, and I'm coming through it, if not out of it. And I've kept it from Dr F. Why? God knows!

I still can't write my chronicle. I tried but I could find no enthusiasm.

Sometimes the dryness comes back in my throat but it isn't there all the time. Just occasionally.

Monday, 20th July

*

Today I went to the shops myself. The terror returned but I made the journey and got back.

Tuesday, 21st July

*

Tomorrow I'll start my account again.

Friday, 31st July

*

There's no point in rewriting what I've relived. Not that
I've heard him again, just that he never went away. I
believed I was over the worst and then the worst arrived.
Now, I think I can keep him at bay long enough to finish
my account.

Sunday, August 2nd

*

Something from way back suggested the Sabbath as a
good day on which to try to find a way of picking up
where I left off twenty-five days ago. It was summer then,
the last summer of my life. It's autumn now, the second
last season of my life. As though he sensed it, Dr F. called
yesterday and stayed a long time – two pots of tea!

He mentioned, as he regularly has, that he's still pursuing some word of Lydia and Myfanwy.

I considered urging him to leave well enough alone,
telling him that I'd abandoned the idea, but resisted. I
gave myself this week to do something, to get back on
track. So today, placing my trust in the Lord I no longer

really believe in, I started writing again. For Abigail. I still owe her this.

*

After James Stubb's departure, the remainder of that afternoon was spent in uncertainty. Everyone wanted to talk about what had happened and what might happen but none seemed willing to do so.

And then, as though God had sent it as a distraction from our hesitancy, a messenger boy arrived by bicycle from Athy post office with a telegram for Joshua. He read it, standing at the kitchen door, while the boy waited in the yard and then he came in, stood at the table, scribbled a reply and gave it to the boy.

Abigail, William, George and I were in the kitchen at the time.

'Sarah has had a seizure, she is ill. I have been sent for. I will travel by train this evening.'

'We are all sorry to hear that,' George said.

'You shouldn't travel alone,' William added.

'Why not?' Joshua asked.

'Because you shouldn't. It's better that someone travels with you, for support.'

'William is right,' Abigail said.

'You and I will go with Joshua,' William said to me. 'If you are willing to come.'

'Of course,' I said.

And in a flurry we prepared and George Carr tacked

the horse and prepared the cart and, within the hour, we were on our journey.

On the train, Joshua asked William what he expected of Sarah's family.

'Not a welcome, I'm sure,' William replied. 'She may wish to see you but they will not. Our company is not meant as an intrusion into your visit, it is meant to sustain.'

Joshua nodded and there was no further conversation for the duration of the journey.

That was my first visit to Dublin but I dared not tell my companions this, it would have been inappropriate.

We reached Sarah Fayle's house late on that May evening. Dusk was falling with the cherry blossoms. The door was opened by a maid who recognized Joshua immediately and ushered him upstairs while we were shown into a parlour. 'I don't trust Sarah's brothers,' William said, pacing the floor.

'Do you think this is a trick, to get Joshua here?'

'Maybe.'

His discomfort soon made me uncomfortable, too, and it came as a relief when Joshua appeared at the door.

'I will stay here tonight,' he said.

'Your wife . . . Sarah . . . isn't well?' William asked.

'No,' Joshua replied, and his voice was hoarse. 'You should find accommodation, there is a lodging house on the next street. I have money.'

William nodded.

'We'll come back here in the morning.'

Joshua seemed not to hear him. While he fumbled in his pocket for money he asked, softly: 'Do we visit our love for one in pain upon another?'

Before we could reply, and what reply was there to give, he found the money, handed it to William and thanked us for our company.

The following morning, we returned to Sarah Fayle's house to find that she was still alive but that she had settled into a torpor in which, her doctor predicted, she might suffer for quite some time but from which she would not recover.

'You should stay as long as you wish to stay,' William urged.

'It is not a time for me to be away from Levitstown,' Joshua replied.

'But it is a time to be with Sarah,' William countered.

This crisis seemed to bring out a strength in William which had long been hinted at but which I had never seen so clearly manifested before.

We were seated in the parlour as this discussion continued when, without warning, and much as one crisis had been overtaken by another the previous afternoon, our discussion was interrupted by the arrival of Sarah's three brothers in the room.

Without introduction or any pleasantries, they set about a verbal assault on Joshua, accusing him of driving their sister to the brink of death, blaming her state on Joshua's wilful disregard for her feelings.

'You allowed her to pursue a business which fed your

egotistical philandering, you abused her goodwill, you dismissed her love as worthless while at the same time continuing as a parasite,' one of them shouted.

'You threw her devotion back in her face and yet you were content to take her money for the support of you and your women,' a second added, gesturing to me.

'You have leached your last off our sister,' the first continued. 'You may have thought you were secure in continuing to drain her life and soul but you are not. If you touch so much as one ha'penny of her money you will suffer every consequences the law can inflict.'

Only then did the third brother, who had towered all this time over Joshua, speak.

'Do not doubt it, Joshua Jacob, for a single moment.'

I think his words, more than those of the other two, struck most fear into us all.

Before Joshua could even consider a reply, the first brother spoke again.

'You may continue under this roof as long as Sarah, in her infirmity, wishes you to but no more than that. And you will never be alone with her. Your camp-followers are no longer welcome.'

With that, the three men left.

We sat in silence a time and then Joshua advised that we should return to Levitstown.

'I will stay here two or three days. If Sarah remains as she is, I will come back then.'

'And if anything happens you will let us know?' I asked.

'I will.'

And so we left Joshua there and returned that evening to our house.

Tuesday, August 4th

*

Yesterday I took my bicycle out and cycled – very slowly and not very far – and felt the better for it.

This morning, just after ten, a man arrived – unannounced – regarding my telephone and by this afternoon I had been connected. The installer ate lunch with me and I enjoyed his company, he was chatty and friendly without being intrusive.

At teatime the telephone rang. I answered in some trepidation. Who could know my number or even know I had a telephone? It was Dr F., ringing to give me his telephone number.

I thanked him for having speeded things up.

Tonight, sitting here, I wondered whether the presence of a telephone would add to the value of the house when it's sold. I've given no thought to that aspect of things, to a will, to whom I should leave the house.

Odd, Ruth lived here for decades and now, within a year, it will change hands twice!

Wednesday, August 5th

*

Today I returned to my task.

*

We were met, at Athy railway station, by John Wickham and your mother. She told us, immediately, that George Carr had left Levitstown the previous day. He had confided to her that he no longer felt he could be part of the White Friends. He insisted, she said, and was at pains to assure her, that his decision had nothing to do with Joshua's intention of divorcing Sarah and marrying her.

'So why did he leave?' William asked.

It was obvious that he was very upset by George's departure. They had become close companions over the months.

'He said he needed a different light, that was all,' Abigail said.

'Likely,' William snorted.

I saw the tears pooling in Abigail's eyes.

'If he has gone it's his decision, not Abigail's,' I said.

'Obviously,' William said, a note of dismissal in his voice. 'Things are decaying. A quarter of our number, near enough, gone in two days.'

I didn't let him continue. 'And they took their own

decisions, they were not forced. Certainly they were not forced by Abigail.'

'I didn't suggest that—'

'Yes, you did,' I interrupted again. 'You think they went because of Joshua's openings and you think they would have stayed if he had not wanted to divorce and marry again. That was his decision. Going was their decision. None of it has a whit to do with Abigail. And if you have a concern about it you had ample time to talk to Joshua when we were travelling to Dublin. And will have again. And if you have a concern with George Carr you should find him and talk to him about it.'

We drove on in silence. Abigail squeezed my arm and I smiled at her. Halfway to Levitstown John Wickham began to speak; his words were from Ecclesiastes but they came out casually, conversationally, and they soothed us all with their compassion.

'To everything there is a season, and a time to every purpose under the heaven: a time to be born, and a time to die; a time to plant, and a time to pluck up that which is planted; a time to kill, and a time to heal; a time to break down, and a time to build up; a time to weep, and a time to laugh; a time to mourn and a time to dance; a time to cast away stones and a time to gather stones together; a time to embrace, and a time to refrain from embracing; a time to get, and a time to lose; a time to keep, and a time to cast away; a time to rend, and a time to sew; a time to keep silence, and a time to speak;

a time to love, and a time to hate; a time of war and a time of peace.'

I missed George Carr greatly. I had great trust in his wisdom and common sense. I was hurt by his departure and by the fact that he left during our absence, without any farewell.

Thursday, August 6th

*

I glanced back through this journal last night, so little about the world outside, so much about the agitation inside me. The weather and the world pass me by, only the intruder comes in. And I look at the telephone, a black crow with its wings folded and its numbers like unblinking eyes, waiting for me to need it. What should be a path to the world outside is only a means to let it know when my decay is almost complete.

Friday, August 7th

*

Joshua returned to us in the first week of June 1899. Sarah had settled into a state of uncertainty, sometimes clear-headed, sometimes befuddled, but free, for the most part, of pain.

We settled, too, into a time of introspection. No one said anything but, I believe, most mornings each secretly counted the others about the table, fearing further losses.

Joshua was most introspective of all and his addresses to us were less certain that they had been, not that he ever turned aside from what had been opened to him.

For Abigail this was a time of great confusion. Her dedication to Joshua was clear. She made no demands on his time or thoughts but she was there when he needed her. At this time, too, despite the burden on our little community, she set about writing a series of letters to your father, her father and a great number of Friends in Rosenallis and Mountmellick. Not a day went by when she did not write two or three letters beseeching people to, at least, let her know where you were. Of the near hundred letters she wrote in that month, only one drew a response. That, she told me, came from a cousin of hers who lived near Mountmellick. I can only guess at the ferocity of its contents for I saw Abigail read it and then, immediately, destroy it.

How she found the energy, day after day, to continue her crusade, to do her work, to attend to Joshua's moods and to be a companion to us I do not know.

*

I expected that Joshua's return would see Abigail move
to his room but this didn't happen. I know she wanted
to but the time and circumstances didn't allow for
it.

Sometimes, in that hot month of June, they escaped
together to the river and sometimes I followed and spied
on them. I told myself it was to protect Abigail. Joshua,
in his uncertain state, was liable to inflict an injury on
her or himself or both of them, so I told myself.

For the most part, their walks were no more than that.
Dour, silent rambles. On a few occasions they kissed and
whispered. Only once, to my knowledge, did austerity
succumb to passion.

That was on a night in the third week of June. In the
oppressive heat none of us found sleep easy, and that
night Abigail crept from our room. She went, without
lighting a candle, through the kitchen and into the yard.
I followed and saw that Joshua was already waiting in
the orchard. They lay together under the trees. I knew
I should leave, and even now, writing this, I still feel a
stinging shame at my prurience. But I was there because
of love and envy. So, instead of leaving, I squatted
among the flowers, watching.

At Joshua's suggestion, she removed her nightgown
and then his and they lay together on the burnt grass.
He talked to her, reminding her that she was the Mother
of the Generations, that God had chosen her, that their
love was consecrated and would be further sanctified in
the years to come. His talk was incessant. Taciturn as

he'd been in the previous weeks, so he was eloquent now. Only Abigail's kisses punctuated his words. I believe strongly, in the light of all that followed, that Joshua was more interested in himself than in others. His talk that night was of the divine, the heavenly, the spiritual, the godly.

Finally, Abigail said fiercely: 'Don't talk about God, show me His love.'

But Joshua would not. Their rendezvous ended shortly afterwards when Abigail would hear no more of the divinity.

'I listen to you, Joshua,' she whispered, 'but I need you to be with me, you must hold me.'

'That time will come,' he said. 'We should not expect it before it's due.'

When I saw Abigail pull her nightdress on, I retreated to our room, getting there only moments before her.

When she got into bed, I pretended sleep and turned and let my hand fall on the chilled skin of her neck. She saw no offence in this familiarity and I took comfort in that.

Saturday, August 8th

*

I remember Abigail's enthusiasm. I try to have it now and sometimes I manage but I find it hard to begin the process. Copying what I've written is the easy part. I enjoy the craft of writing, not the art of remembering.

*

Apart from your mother's enthusiasm and Joshua's moodiness, the other thing I remember about that month of June in Levitstown was the peace of not going out preaching. The people we met were the people who came to us, not the people we went in search of in the market places.

We settled into a routine life. We rose and ate and worked in the mornings. After lunch, because of the great heat of that month, we sat in the house, reading or talking. In the late afternoon we worked again and in the evening, after we had eaten and prayed, we entertained ourselves.

I recall Ann Fox giving your mother and me great amusement with a children's book of instruction she was writing. Its purpose was to make reading and writing and arithmetic easier for children. The means was to instil rhymes that the children could remember.

One that gave us much laughter was a rhyme Ann had concocted to help children count backwards from twenty to nought. I don't recall it all but I have never forgotten the last verses.

> *Fifteen, fourteen, thirteen, twelve, eleven,*
> *ten, nine, eight and seven;*
> *six and five and four,*

> *then three and two and just one more;*
> *and that one is one*
> *and then it's done.*

Ann would read these verses to us as we worked in the kitchen and we would try to keep straight faces, imagining how children would react when faced with her ingenious and convoluted method.

In the evenings, Abigail, William and I helped John with his watering and weeding in the garden. Not an evening went but five or six callers came to see John, to seek his horticultural advice or simply to chat with him and enjoy his common sense and good humour.

I loved these hours of listening and talking and always resented the darkness that, finally, drove us inside.

And then, in the third week of June, Joshua seemed to rouse himself from his lethargy and he informed us that he had had another opening, while walking the road between Levitstown and Maganey, and that the Lord had instructed him that guidance would be found in the random opening of the Bible.

So, every evening, after our meal, Joshua casually opened the Bible and read the verses his eye fell upon.

The first evening the verse was from Isaiah, regarding the sinful nation. The second came from Nehemiah and concerned the gates of Jerusalem burning. The third was from Joel and I could not contain my merriment when Joshua solemnly read it to us.

'Awake, ye drunkards, and weep; and howl, all ye

drinkers of wine, because of the new wine; for it is cut off from your mouth.'

Whether it was the insult of my levity or a growing enthusiasm for the sound of his own voice, Joshua spoke for almost an hour, referring to our vines, to the sin of drunkenness, to the dangers and opportunities offered by the Lord, of the importance of accepting that what we desire is not always what we receive.

And while he droned on I could see the sun shining across from the elbow of the river and the old men whose stories I loved, whose voices reminded me of my grandfather, gathering in the garden and I wanted to be out there with them.

For me, these readings were an inconvenience. For William they were a misery. He felt this haphazard choice of verses was dangerous.

'Are we to be guided now by the turn of a page, are we come down to that?' he asked one evening at the end of that week. We were sitting in the garden, Abigail and William and I, the fruit and vegetables watered.

'The Lord has written all the words,' Abigail said. 'It isn't simply random reading, it's all the word of God.'

'It's childish,' William answered and the brevity of his statement made me suspect that he would not long be with us.

The following morning, when the chance arose, I tackled him about this. He didn't deny the possibility.

'If I asked James Stubb to stay,' I told him, 'then I'm begging you to remain.'

'Why?' he asked.

'Because your loss would be the loss of everything. You are more important to the White Friends than you imagine. If only for us, stay here, at least another month. Give me your word. If Joshua's readings are a madness, give it time to pass. In the meantime, we need you.'

He thought for a time and then he agreed.

'A month,' he said. 'I can promise no more.'

Sunday, August 9th

*

Today I cycled out the Stradbally road but when I was no more than a mile from Athy I felt a tinge of pain beginning and returned slowly. However, after a rest, the pain passed and I contented myself with reading the papers and walking to the Park after tea.

On the way back, I met Dr F. and told him what had happened. He made me swear I'd phone him if the pain returned.

'We may have to increase your medication if that happens,' he told me.

I must have looked concerned because he added: 'But then, that's what it's for.'

Monday, August 10th

*

Today was painless and productive. Which says much for my improved disposition.

*

Each time we faced a crisis in our community, Sarah Fayle seemed to take a hand in its resolution. The Monday after Joshua had begun his random readings he was again sent for because of her illness.

This time he travelled alone and was gone but three days.

Again, in his absence, we were a more settled community. It seemed to me that we might, in the long run, prove much steadier and more sturdy under William's less singular but more stable leadership.

I said this to him and he did not balk at the proposal.

'But Joshua was the fire that led us all here. I'm not sure how we might manage without that fire,' he said. 'I could never match his inspiration. I only wish he was not leading us so erratically.'

I knew, of course, that your mother would not share my opinion. Nor would the Fox sisters. I did broach the subject with John Wickham one morning as we worked in the garden.

'The sparrow finds a house and the wren a nest,' John

said. *'Jesus provides and it's our part to uncover his provisions.'*

*

Years afterwards, it struck me that this was the only occasion during my time with the White Friends that I'd heard the name of Jesus, a more personal and a warmer name than Lord, mentioned.

*

From the little information Joshua was willing to give on his return, we gleaned that Sarah had once more returned from death's door.

We were also aware of the fact that Joshua had brought with him a good deal of money. There was no secret about this.

Joshua had returned to us on Thursday, the twenty-second day of June, and the following Tuesday he took all of us, apart from John Wickham, to Athy and preached at the market there.

This, coming after weeks of lethargy, was a startling return to our earlier days of going out among the people. We were hard pressed to discover where our pamphlets were stored but Joshua was enlivened at the prospect and he preached as I had never heard him preach before. His voice rang about the market square. His theme, in the early part of his preaching, was hellfire and brimstone but at one point this changed to the love of God and the need to look for the good in all people.

147

He retold the parable of the mustard seed and, in his telling, love was the least of seeds and the greatest of herbs without which our lives were flavourless.

Late in the afternoon, as the crowds were melting from the square, Joshua saw some lawyers leaving the Court House, across the street from where we were standing.

The court had been in session that day and the sight of these men in their wigs and gowns drew a torrent from Joshua regarding whited sepulchres and the work of the Devil.

'The only law is the law of God,' he boomed. 'Those who live by Caesar's law spit in the face of the Lord, who created the only true law. Read Psalms and you will read the truth, the only delight is in the law of the Lord, there is no other law.'

Such was the contempt in Joshua's tone, so obvious was his target, that it was no surprise when, within minutes, we were faced by a column of policemen. They in turn were followed by a crowd of townspeople, most of whom had never listened to Joshua but who were fascinated by the sudden confrontation.

The arrival of the policemen seemed to incense Joshua even further.

'Do you come in the name of Caesar, do you face the Words of God with batons, do you believe for an instant that you are doing anything other than the work of the Devil? You may silence me but you will not silence the Lord our Father, who sees what you do.'

That was the last we heard from Joshua. He was bun-

dled away between three rugged policemen, one of whom firmly clasped his mouth in the palm of an enormous hand.

As this was happening, William quietly ushered us around the corner and away from the policemen, guiding us through the crowd so that, even in our distinctive garb, we were difficult to identify. The crowd, having no sympathy for the police, did their part in hiding us.

The police, having silenced their adversary, obviously saw no point in provoking the crowd and marched away in the direction of their barracks.

We gathered on the river bank and William ordered us to go home, as quickly and innocuously as possible. He would visit the barracks and then follow us. Abigail was for going with him and, eventually, he gave in to her.

Mary and Ann Fox and I, leaving the horse and cart with William and Abigail, walked along the river bank until we were clear of the town. Only then did we come back onto the roadway.

It was almost dark when William and Abigail reached home. Their news was not good. Joshua was being kept in the barracks and would be charged with intimidation and disturbance of the peace.

Later, when William and I had a moment together, his anger became obvious.

'I tried to reason with Joshua but he never missed a chance to berate the policemen. It was hopeless. He wants to be there, to be imprisoned. He's mad.'

*

He was angry, too, with Abigail who would hear nothing said against Joshua. She rounded on the police sergeant, and on the journey home she accused William of not being committed to the White Friends.

'I can't listen to him and her castigating me when neither of them knows where we're going. To Abigail he's God and I think he believes that of himself, too.'

*

'What made him turn on those lawyers?' I asked.

William shrugged. 'The chance to be a martyr, to be glorified?'

'He is anxious about Sarah. And her brothers,' I suggested.

'And yet there's the money he brought back. That must have come from Sarah's business. There's no reason in any of this, Elizabeth. It becomes more insane as he does.'

'And will you go?' I asked.

'I won't desert him in his madness, no.'

'And you won't desert us?'

'I gave you my word that I'd stay,' he answered.

I was glad to number him friend, for such he was. There was much about William that irked me but much more that I loved.

*

I tried to talk sense to Abigail, to explain that she mustn't antagonize people any more than need be but, as William had said, she was staunch in her support of Joshua.

'The Lord speaks through him,' she said.

I wanted to repeat her words from the orchard, to remind her that she, too, had wished for more than talk about the love of God but I couldn't and wouldn't.

Tuesday, August 11th

*

Today I wrote, cycled and enjoyed the day.

*

I expected, I think we all did, that Joshua would be released in a short time from the barrack prison in Athy but this did not happen.

William and Abigail and I went to visit him there the following morning and John and the Fox sisters travelled in the following day but there was no sign of his release. Instead, we were told, he would appear at the court in Castledermot on the following Wednesday. In the meantime, all we could do was bring him food, encourage him and pray for him.

On the Thursday, John and the Fox sisters reported that there were several people in the vicinity of the barracks and that they had been drawn there by Joshua's preaching through the bars of his cell.

*When, on the Friday, William and Abigail and I trav-
elled to see him, we were met by a crowd of twenty-five
or thirty people. Joshua's voice rang out through the hot,
dry air. His text was from Judges, regarding the imprisonment of Samson.*

*' "But the Philistines took him, and put out his eyes,
and brought him down to Gaza, and bound him with
fetters of brass; and he did grind in the prison house," '
he shouted.*

*A few people among the listeners jeered but, to my
surprise, a number – including two well-dressed women
– stood in silence, listening. It was to these that Joshua
addressed himself.*

*'To be imprisoned does not make me a prisoner; to be
bound hand and foot does not make me a captive; to be
locked away in an asylum does not make me insane; to
be branded troublemaker does not deny the peace within
me.*

*'I am free; I am loosed; I am wise; I am a peacemaker.
I come in the light of the Lord with His words on my lips
and His love in my heart.'*

*His face, bearded and tanned, framed by the bars, and
his voice, reasoning with the onlookers, made him an
admirable figure.*

*When we went inside, however, the picture was not so
noble. His cell was hot and stank. His eyes, despite their
brightness, were circled with black and his back was
stooped.*

We fed him and prayed with him and then left Abigail with him for a time.

While we waited for her to join us, the sergeant of the barracks came and stood with us.

'Your friend would be better served in keeping silent until he is dealt with,' he said.

He appeared a reasonable man and William seemed sympathetic to his words.

'I couldn't care a whit what you do or don't believe,' the sergeant continued. 'But this preaching and drawing a rabble to the barracks will not do him any good when he appears before the Justice. Trouble enough to beard the lawyers outside the court but this is pouring oil on a blazing fire. Can you not advise him against this course?'

William assured him that we would try.

'Try,' the sergeant sighed. 'Prison is not the place for your companion but he seems determined to remain locked up.'

When your mother emerged, William went back and talked with Joshua but his discussion was fruitless and, as we drove away, his voice, again, rang out behind us.

That night, Joshua was removed to the more secure prison in the police barracks in Carlow. There he was unable to preach, having no access to a window. And there we visited him on Saturday and Sunday.

On the Sunday, one of the women who had been among the crowd at Athy was waiting outside the barracks and approached us as we went in.

'You are visiting Joshua Jacob?' she enquired.

William nodded.

'If he should need assistance, if he should need the services of a lawyer, it can be arranged.'

'That is very generous,' William said. 'To whom do we owe this generous offer?'

'I'm here on behalf of Catherine Devine,' the woman said.

'And Joshua knows her?'

She nodded.

'Would you like to accompany us inside?' I asked.

She hesitated and then shook her head.

'I can give him your message,' William said. 'Where can you or Miss Devine be contacted?'

'I'll wait here,' the woman said.

We delivered the message but Joshua dismissed the idea immediately.

' "Then one of them, which was a lawyer, asked Him a question, tempting Him," ' he quoted Matthew. 'We will have no truck with lawyers. Thank her but tell her I will be defended by the Lord.'

And so we did and she went away.

Through all of this visit Abigail never spoke and that night a terrible sickness took hold of her and she became fevered and began to rant and rage about you, about Joshua, about the bars she imagined on the window of our room, about never seeing her father again.

All that night and the next day and the following night, we took it in turns to sit with her, for she could *not be left alone. Several times each day and night we changed the sodden sheets from the bed.*

Late on Tuesday night William returned from Carlow. John Wickham and Ann Fox had retired, and Mary Fox was watching over Abigail, so I sat with William and he told me that he had encountered Sarah Devine at the barracks.

'She was there with another offer of help for tomorrow.'

'Who is she?' I asked.

'She is a wealthy woman from Athy. She was one of the crowd outside his cell when we visited him there.'

'And is she a believer?'

He shook his head.

'I spoke to her as I left. She sang Joshua's praises, said he's a wonderful man. I asked her if she was a White Friend but she said she wasn't.'

'So why is she eager to help?'

A shrug and a wry smile.

'Which is what Abigail needs,' I said sarcastically.

'Which is what all of us need,' William sighed.

William and John travelled, the following day, to Castledermot and returned with the news that Joshua had been remanded back to Carlow until the following week.

'And was Miss Devine there?' I asked.

'Mrs Devine,' William corrected me. 'Yes, she was.'

'She's married, then?'

'Widowed.'

*

At the time, the thought crossed my mind that if Catherine Devine lured Joshua away then I might have Abigail to myself. But that was to do her a great injustice, for deep as my devotion was to Abigail, her devotion to Joshua was deeper than I could have imagined.

Wednesday, August 12th

*

The last days have been good ones. I know I float and sink by turns, that neither my optimism nor my black pessimism are reality, though what reality is in the face of death, God only knows. But while this floating optimism – not optimism, acceptance – remains I've set myself a task. Apart from completing this account.

I've chosen Saturday next, August 15th, my seventyninth birthday, as the day when I'll complete the task! Intrigue!

*

Catherine Devine became a daily visitor to Joshua while he was in Carlow barracks. Whenever one of our number went to visit him, she was there or had been there. On the one occasion when I met her, she was pleasant.

My concern at that time, however, was less with Joshua and Catherine Devine and more with your mother. Twice in that week we called the doctor from

Athy and, despite his best efforts, your mother continued in a state of fevered confusion.

I was convinced that nothing, short of your return, would cure her. She talked about you all the time. Sometimes her talk was coherent and sometimes rambling but there was seldom a time in that sickness when your names were not on her tongue.

On the Saturday of that week, the 8th of July, John Wickham and I left Levitstown early and journeyed to Mountmellick. I was determined to speak to your grandfather and had convinced the others that it was our only hope if we were to save Abigail from the derangement which threatened her mind and the sickness that wasted her body. She had, it appeared, given up on life. I believed that your presence would be the tonic to make her want to live again. So I went in search of Abigail's father, believing he would give me word of your whereabouts.

I believed, I didn't dare think otherwise, that when his daughter's illness was explained your grandfather would immediately contact you. I allowed myself to visualize the scene. You coming quietly into the room, your mother opening her eyes and recognizing you, the change in her would be immediate.

On that journey, I thought of nothing else. The reconciliation would occur within days. Nothing mattered apart from your mother's health.

*

In that I'm not entirely truthful. Already, I believed that Joshua was more concerned with his ego than with the illness of his wife or the woman who loved him. I gave no thought to him at all. I saw Lydia and Myfanwy's presence as the beginning of Abigail's recovery. With her returning strength she'd see the futility of expecting a life with Joshua. She and Lydia and Myfanwy and I would find a life together.

I was young, I was in love. What other excuse can I offer for my blind confidence?

*

But I was to learn, very quickly, that I could not undo the rejection that Abigail's departure had fastened. Nothing, I believe, could have brought about a reconciliation. Abigail might have gone on bended knee, in sackcloth, to her father's door and he would have closed it in her face.

I found him, I spoke to him, I told him of her condition, I explained that she was slipping away and that she might soon be gone from us if something was not done to save her.

He sat, that obdurate old man, and listened and then he dismissed me.

'You are mistaken, young woman.' he said. 'I have no daughter and there is nothing I can do.'

At that, my tears streamed and I begged him to at least give me some indication as to where I might contact your father or to undertake to contact him for me.

'*The whereabouts of my son-in-law and his children is of no concern to you, it has no bearing on the condition of your friend.*'

John Wickham, who had remained in silence throughout, rose from his seat and crossed to where your grandfather sat.

'*"Full well ye reject the commandment of God, that ye may keep your own tradition." You will find that verse in Mark, in the word of God,*' *John said and then shook his head slowly.* '*I have no daughter, but if I had I could not wish for a better daughter than Abigail. I will do my best to be a father to her but I cannot be child to her, too. And I cannot save her, that's a gift in your giving.*'

Your grandfather looked shaken but he did not relent and we left. I was in tears and John Wickham shook with anger.

We made enquiries about Mountmellick but there was no one willing or able to help us in our search for you.

We travelled through that night, a hot night, well lit by a near-full moon, and reached Levitstown in the early dawn of that Sabbath, the ninth day of July, 1899. That was the last time I tried to find you. I hope I am more successful in this attempt.

*

That does little justice to the coldness of Abigail's father or to the heartfelt words of John Wickham who came closer than anyone to shaking the hateful old man out of his iciness. God forbid that his character might have skipped a generation to his grandchildren. Perish the thought!

Thursday, August 13th

*

There's so little about life, life as it goes on, as it passes me by, as it sometimes involves me, in this diary. No one appears any more – the Murphys, the people I meet in the street, even myself as I am. Its concern is the distant past. But there is life going on. The Murphys come and go. I see Dr Fullard regularly. Life happens in Offaly Street. The market happens. I get to know people. And that's important to record. And the fine weather stretches into August!

*

Our return journey to Levitstown was a sombre one, but in the last mile home John Wickham brightened.

'If her father won't save Abigail then we must,' he said.

'But can we?' I asked and it was an earnest question, for I believed that if John Wickham considered your mother's salvation to be in our power then it was.

'We can.' He nodded.

And we set about it at once.

That day, he and I carried Abigail outside and placed

her in a chair in the orchard. John worked close to where she sat and never ceased to converse with her. And when his old cronies came in the evening they, too, sat with her and talked to her.

'If she die, it will not be alone or for want of solace,' John said that night, when William questioned the wisdom of moving her about in her condition.

On Monday and Tuesday we did the same thing, refusing to allow her to recline in her room, bringing her out where the sun shone and life went on and work was done.

On Wednesday morning, William woke me. He had gone to check on Abigail before setting out for Castledermot court and found her awake and alert, her fever greatly reduced.

'It's a good omen.' William smiled. 'This may be a good day for all of us.'

Later, remembering that morning and William's optimism, I counted it one of the worst days of Abigail's life. It was the day when Joshua was fined in court and his fine was paid by Catherine Devine. It was the day when he came back to us in some triumph. It was the day when Abigail was well enough to welcome his return and celebrate with us. But it was the day, too, I'm convinced, when Joshua turned from us and seriously considered another path.

Friday, August 14th

*

The week has flowed by and now I'm on the brink of doing what I set myself to do. I won't say what, because if I write it I may not do it.

So, back to work.

*

Joshua returned to us on the evening of his release. He was accompanied by William and Catherine Devine and another woman, a friend of Catherine's, whose name I don't recall.

They ate with us and the conversation was good-humoured. Joshua referred, several times, to Catherine Devine's generosity in paying his fine and she, in turn, urged him not to ruin her financially by being arrested again.

I expected him to answer her with some reminder that the word of the Lord would not be silenced but he did not.

For the rest of that week, and through the following, Joshua remained in Levitstown. He was attentive to Abigail and her strength returned. Indeed, her colour surpassed my own, and as she took the sun her skin darkened and her eyes recovered their glow.

One evening, when Joshua was writing in his room, she and I walked slowly, arm in arm, to the river.

'I remember nothing of my sickness,' she told me. 'Other than the terror of the deprivation and destitution I felt for my children. More than anything, more than sickness or Joshua's imprisonment or anything. I wanted my children. That's a craving that will never lessen.'

She turned to me, then, and her eyes fastened on mine and there was no escaping them.

'I will get them back, won't I?' she asked.

'You will,' I said and I believed it.

The following Sunday, the twenty-third day of July, Joshua's wife, Sarah Fayle, died. Word reached him early on Monday morning and he left, immediately, for Dublin.

During his absence, a period of three days, Abigail seemed to find a new lease of life. The weight of Sarah's illness and Joshua's bind were lifted and with them went the remnants of Abigail's listlessness.

'At least that difficulty is removed,' William said. 'We need not fear the wrath of Joshua's divorce. Sarah Fayle has been generous to us. Again.'

'And what of Mrs Devine?' I asked.

William sighed.

'That was a fear, wasn't it, but Joshua has been mindful of Abigail since his release.'

'He has,' I said. 'But I don't trust him.'

'Why?'

'Very well, then,' I said. 'I don't trust her. Them. I don't trust them.'

'I believe we were wrong.' William smiled. 'Maybe you and I are too suspicious. We have no reason to be. Catherine hasn't appeared since his release. Maybe she's simply a generous person and he's simply relieved to be back among us. Maybe the worst is over.'

'Do you think so?'

He nodded and grinned but I thought it an uneasy grin.

Saturday, August 15th

*

I woke this morning to my seventy-ninth birthday. I'd slept well last night and the day was as glorious as all the others this week. There's no sign of autumn and even the evenings remain stretched by the clear skies and late sun.

I'd hardly finished breakfast when the Murphys arrived with a box of chocolates and a birthday card. Despite my questioning, they wouldn't divulge how they knew my birth date. However, within the hour the answer arrived, in the shape of Dr Fullard – flowers and a record of famous overtures in hand.

'And I have another present,' he told me, as we drank coffee and ate the cakes he'd brought.

'This is an embarrassment,' I told him. 'I've learned to forget birthdays.'

'That's not a philosophy I subscribe to at all,' Dr F. said, shaking his head. 'Now, this may not come to too much but I think I've traced one of your friend's daughters.'

Suddenly, I was trembling.

Dr F. rose and came around the table and put his hands on my shoulders.

'I should have been more circumspect in telling you.'

'No.' I shook my head but I couldn't find words to express my gratitude.

'I think it's her, you understand that,' he said. 'There's a chance that my information is wrong but I'm pretty sure it's not. I wanted to be certain before I told you but I'm sure enough to take a chance on it.'

'Thank you,' I said.

'I need another week to confirm it.'

'How?' I asked.

'How did I find her?'

I nodded.

'Medical records. But I'm having it checked out by a colleague who lives near her. He's away on holiday until the middle of next week.'

So the first half of this day ended on a high note. I know it may be too high, overflowing with expectations, but there is hope and purpose where yesterday there was only a vague prospect.

Fortified with this happiness, I set about my task for today.

Early in the afternoon, I took out my bicycle, made enquiries at O'Brien's shop and cycled up the long avenue that brought me into a courtyard, surrounded by old low sheds and workshops. Here, immediately, I came face to face with the man I was seeking. The undertaker whose voice and face have haunted me for so long. That voice: as soon as he spoke it filled my head but I gripped the handlebars of my bicycle, thought of the kindnesses of the morning, the generosity of the Murphys and Dr F. and refused to be frightened – or, at least, to surrender to my fear.

'Can I help you?' the man asked.

'Yes,' I said. 'You can stop haunting me.'

He looked at me as though I was completely insane.

'I don't think I know who you are,' he said.

I wheeled my bicycle towards him and I noticed that he stepped back a half-step. I offered my hand.

'My name is Elizabeth Hallhead.'

He took my hand, but warily.

I won't say I was enjoying his discomfort but I was more in control than he.

'We met once,' I continued. 'Outside the bakery. You offered to help me across the street. I was less than grateful. I was frightened then.'

He nodded and I could see the confirmation of my insanity in his head.

'Really? Why?'

166

'Because I realized you were the undertaker, my undertaker.'

His brow furrowed.

'I'm dying,' I said. It was the first time I've said that out loud and it sounded matter of fact, even to my ears. 'I've known this for some time but when I heard you in the bakery, when I realized you'd be the one, it terrified me. I came out here today to meet you, to face you. To face myself.'

'I see.'

Still he was uncertain.

'I'm not mad,' I said, trying to put him at ease.

'Of course not,' he laughed but his laugh was nervous and his tone didn't convince me.

'Look,' I said, as matter-of-factly as I could. 'The shadow of death makes some strange shapes and one of mine was the fear of you. In the end, I thought I'd better meet you and prove to myself that you're not an ogre. And anyway, I need to make arrangements with you, to do business. You are the only local undertaker?'

He nodded.

'A one-hearse town,' I said.

He burst out laughing and his laughter and then mine seemed to dispel the tension between us.

He invited me into his office and then took me through the empty workshop and showed me his coffins. By late this afternoon I had chosen mine. A plain, unadorned box. No handles, no crosses, no carvings. And no frills inside. I was insistent on that!

167

I cycled home with the undertaker's birthday wishes in my ears and with a sense of triumph, not over death but over the fear of life.

Elizabeth Hallhead, I'm proud of you!

In spite of many things and because of some people this has been a happy, happy birthday. I spent a very contented hour before retiring, listening to the record Dr F. brought this morning. *Figaro*; *William Tell*; *The Merry Wives of Windsor*; *Russlan* and *Ludmilla*; *Tannhäuser* and *Die Fledermaus*.

Sunday, August 16th

*

Which daughter has Dr F. tracked down? That question remains. I never thought to ask him and, in a way, I don't want to know, not yet. Let that mystery remain.

To begin my eightieth year with reasonable health (for now) is not so bad, I suppose. At least my faculties are intact. For small mercies let us be thankful!

My funeral is arranged and will be paid for in the coming week. I'll leave the receipts and information with Mrs Murphy and Dr F. I can be brought directly from here to the burial ground in Ballitore.

If the weather and my strength hold, I've planned another task for next Saturday. One that has been a constant in my head, one I've saved as a child would save a treat.

So, to today's work.

*

In the short period of tranquillity that followed Joshua's return, your mother grew in strength and happiness and hope. Her conviction that she would see you again strengthened with her general optimism. None of us had the heart to tell her of the outcome of our journey to see your grandfather. Indeed, the journey was never mentioned to Joshua or Abigail. There was no point in damping her enthusiasm for life and William and I feared what use Joshua would make of the information. For all we knew, it might end up as fodder for a sermon.

To see Abigail's strength and verve return lifted our hearts. Her laughter haunted the garden and her energy was boundless. She spent long hours with John Wickham, assisting him in his every task. No matter what the problems he faced, she was quick to suggest a solution and no matter how difficult the duty involved she was first to undertake it. She enjoyed her work and her enjoyment was infectious. Our days passed in happiness.

John and William and Abigail and I looked after the garden. Ann and Mary Fox cooked and cleaned the house. Joshua spent most of his time in reading and writing. But even he seemed to have a more settled manner.

At the end of the first week of August, however, Joshua

*called us together and informed us that the Lord had
opened to him again. He told us he had been ordered to
spend forty days and forty nights in prayer. He quoted
at length from the Testament, his voice thundering and
resounding as it had done in the market places, his
pauses thrown dramatically before us.*

'*It rained for forty days and nights in Noah's time;
at the end of forty days Noah opened the window on
the ark; Moses was on the mountain forty days and
nights; Elijah spent forty days on Mount Horeb; the
iniquity of the house of Judah was borne for forty days;
after forty days Nineveh was overthrown; the Lord fasted
for forty days and nights and remained with the disciples
forty days after His resurrection. So, when He opened to
me that I should go away from here and spend that time
in prayer and meditation, I knew it was of the greatest
importance. It will be a time of preparation for a great
change that is to come.*'

*Without looking, I knew that William's brow was
already furrowed in concern at the prophetic path Joshua
had laid for himself. My more immediate concern was
with Abigail but she seemed to accept the news blithely.*

'*Nothing comes without pain,*' *Joshua continued.* '*We
have lived here in a time of trial and a time of peace but
the time ahead will be a time when God will make His
will finally known. None of us walks entirely in the
Light. Each of us is blighted by sin. We are the children
of Adam and Eve. Our eyes are opened and we see our
nakedness and we sew fig leaves together in which to go*

about. But a time is coming, as Isaiah foretold, when the leaves will fall as the leaves of the oak tree do. And then we shall be as the fig tree in the Lord's parable. "When her branch is yet tender, and putteth forth leaves, ye know that summer is near." So our summer and our time will be nigh. I have faith in my God and I have faith that He will guide me finally to the door which hides all secrets and He will gift me the key to that door.'

'It is the will of God,' Ann Fox said.

*

Again, my mind turned to the possibilities which Joshua's absence created. I recognized this as probably the last time I would have Abigail to myself and I determined not to fritter the opportunity to, at least, let her know my feelings. I had no idea how I'd do this but that evening, listening to Joshua droning on and placing himself in a direct line from Genesis to the four gospels, I felt I'd been given another chance. The thought crossed my mind, and I smiled at it, that perhaps this was indeed the will of God, that Abigail and myself should be together. Perhaps Joshua's opening was entirely for my benefit!

*

I made it my business to question Abigail that night but she seemed perfectly at ease with Joshua's absence.

'I believe I know the change that will come,' she said.

171

'He will grieve for Sarah, he must grieve for her. They were man and wife for such a long time, no loss goes unfelt, none. He will come back with his heart and soul in order.'

'You don't believe he's had an opening, then?'

'I don't know,' Abigail said quietly. 'I only know he needs to put that life to rest before he begins another.'

'With you?'

She smiled.

'With all of us. It will be a good life. We mustn't protect what we have. We must give it freely to everyone who wishes to share it. It's not a light to be hidden under a bushel.'

*

Will you share your light with me? I wondered. Will you love me the way you love Joshua? Will you lie in the orchard with me and invite my kisses? I want you to.

I told myself I'd ask her when Joshua was gone. Then, I told myself, then I'll do it. Then.

*

Joshua Jacob left Levitstown on the morning of the fifteenth of August 1899. It was my nineteenth birthday but that fact was lost in the excitement of his going.

We saw him off from the gateway. He hugged each of us in turn and promised that we would be in his thoughts. He left us in the care of William and promised he would see us late in September.

'Wherever God takes me, and I know not where that may be, He will make His purpose known for us, whatever that design may be,' Joshua said and then he hoisted his bag on his back and set off along the roadway. We remained where we were and, at the bend in the road, he turned and waved to us and we waved back. And then he was gone from our sight.

For a short time, we stood in the gateway, as if expecting his reappearance. Eventually, William and John broke away from our little knot and they were followed by the Fox sisters. I stayed with Abigail for a little while before leaving her to her own thoughts. Later, she joined us in the kitchen and, whatever sadness was in her, she put it away and set enthusiastically about the day's business.

In the afternoon, my parents arrived from Ballitore with gifts for my birthday and stayed for dinner. It was a happy day to be there with family and Friends.

Monday, August 17th

*

We've been blessed with the warm weather of this month and it goes on unabated and with no a sign of breaking. I listen, avidly, every day to the weather forecast but it continues to promise an Indian summer.

I get out, walking the Barrow track every day, and I write in the afternoon. In the evening, I copy my account into this diary.

I could live to enjoy this routine.

*

After Joshua left for his forty days of prayer, we spent a few days in our routine work and then your mother suggested that we should turn our thoughts to continuing the work he had begun. She proposed that we return to preaching at the markets in Athy and Carlow. The Fox sisters were enthusiastic, though neither was prepared to preach. William did not dismiss the idea and John Wickham said he would support us if we deemed it the right thing to do.

I was dubious about the idea. Our recent troubles did not encourage me to go back into the public market place.

We discussed the suggestion a great deal and, finally, it was agreed that we would go to Athy and Carlow on the market days of the following week and that William and Abigail would preach, while Ann and Mary Fox and I distributed our literature.

I remember my nervousness, fear, travelling to Athy on market morning. I was sure that we would all be imprisoned immediately but the day passed quietly. William preached but his style was stiff and of little interest to those in search of entertainment.

Your mother was much more impressive – and a revelation to us all. Rather than preparing a sermon, Abigail opened her Bible at will, as Joshua had done of late, and read the passage that fell to her, which was 1 Timothy 1:5. She spoke on charity and the pure heart and true faith.

'The pure heart,' she told her listeners, 'can accept the deepest hurt. The pure heart is charitable because charity is the greatest gift you can offer. True faith is all that matters because the reward of faith is truth in the Lord.'

When she spoke her voice was never raised but there was an intensity, a sincerity, that was missing from Joshua's sermonizing.

Again, in Carlow, she chose a passage at random and spoke with candour and without artifice. Her belief in what she was saying was enough to carry her through.

The intensity of Joshua's haranguing, which by its very tone drew hostility, was replaced by the quiet honesty of Abigail's words. The crowds about us were smaller but they stayed to listen.

*

And how beautiful she looked. I'd stand watching her, forgetting my work, only passing out our pamphlets when someone requested them. I'd watch her, the strong sun falling on her tanned face; her hair tied up, catching the tunnels of the sunlight; her eyes holding the attention of the people about her; her white dress folding around her slim figure. I was enraptured. Just to see her there, to be in her presence, was enough. In those public places, I was proud to be in her company. Her friendship was much more important to me than the White Friends.

I wanted to hold her, to be held by her. As I still do.

*

We returned to Athy and Carlow in the last week of August and, again, Abigail preached and people listened.

Journeying home from those outings, William joked that he should stay in Levitstown, and help John Wickham, while the White Women, as he called us, got on with the business of preaching and handing out pamphlets.

On the morning after our second visit to Carlow market, talking with William while we worked in the garden, I realized that his hopes were higher than they had been in a long time.

'Our numbers are small,' he admitted, 'but they will grow and it's better that they grow slowly, that people come because they understand what we are about.'

That afternoon, it was a Friday, as we finished our midday meal, a horse and trap turned into the yard.

Ann Fox went to see who might be calling and returned to the kitchen, where we were still sitting about the table, followed by a man whom I didn't immediately recognize. But your mother did and her face whitened, as though it had been turned to alabaster.

As the man stood at the head of the table, I saw that

it was your father, Robert Beale. That recognition brought a moment of delight. I believed, foolishly, that your grandfather had had a change of heart and persuaded Robert to make his peace with Abigail and to return you to her. As soon as he opened his mouth, however, my hopes were shattered.

'I've come to take you away from here, Abigail,' he said, and his tone was tart and harsh.

Had he asked for time alone with your mother we would gladly have given it but the curt way in which he addressed her and his discourtesy in ignoring us, into whose home he had marched uninvited, determined us to stay. Our presence, however, seemed of no consequence to him.

'For what reason?' Abigail asked.

'You have frittered months away on this stupidity. You have put your health at risk. You have abandoned your children and neglected me. You have distressed your father. And you have cavorted and made a fool of yourself with this laughing-stock.'

He looked about the kitchen and only then realized that Joshua was not present. Nevertheless he continued.

'You have done all this for your own recreation but the time for such is over. I can never forgive the hurt you have done but I am prepared to allow you to resume your role as mother to your children. You will come with me.'

At that, your mother rose from her chair and spoke slowly, calmly and with enormous courage to this man who had come to bully, embarrass and torment her.

'I will not come with you, Robert Beale, now or ever. You were the one who denied my existence. You were the one who buried me in your hard heart. You cannot keep my children from me, they will always be mine and I will always be theirs and there's nothing you can do to hinder that, no matter how you try. Lydia and Myfanwy are my daughters and distance and time will never alter the fact. Ever.'

She rounded the table and stood face to face with your father.

'You disowned me, you ignored my pleadings and my letters, you left me in misery. And now you think you can threaten and intimidate me but you can't. Never again. You have nothing that I need. My children are my children and that is all that matters and you can waste your life trying to keep them from me but it will be a waste because we share the same blood and love.'

She stepped back then and spoke very quietly and there was a grittiness in her character that your father's bullying could never match.

'I have no notion why you came here today but whoever you were seeking she is not here. You were the one who said that in the first place. Now, get out.'

With that, Abigail turned and left the kitchen, closing our bedroom door behind her.

Your father stood a moment in the kitchen and then he, too, turned and left. None of us followed but we heard the horse and trap in the yard and then the clop of the

*hoofs and the rolling of the wheels faded on the open
road.*

*I may be hard on your father in what I have written
but that visit was devoid of any care or love or tenderness. Had your father wished to win your mother back
he might have come with an open mind, a resolution not
to hurt and humiliate her. Instead, he came to do just
that. To frighten and overwhelm her. I have no doubt
that he came as a result of the visit John Wickham and
I paid to your grandfather. He waited a time and then,
believing your mother was at too low an ebb to resist,
came to cow her.*

*The man you knew, grew up with and loved as a
father may have been kindness itself to you and it is not
my intention to try to destroy that memory. But the man
who dealt with your mother in that troubled time showed
no compassion, no understanding, no willingness to listen. Always, his was the final word. Did he think he
could chase Abigail back into the life she had led? Was
he more concerned with his own pride than he was with
your need for a mother? Was it his intention to restore
his own standing as a husband and upright Friend by
dragging your mother back, against her will?*

The answer to each of these questions is yes.

*His actions showed him to be the overbearing, cow-
ardly and self-righteous man your mother could not love.
She was thrice cursed in the men about her. Your grandfather disowned his daughter; your father ignored the*

needs of his wife; and Joshua Jacob rejected the woman whose love was more than he deserved.

Query what I have written, if you like, but I have written it in the belief that it is true.

*

I read this back and I know it will cause pain but, in a way, I feel that it should for it came out of a far greater pain and Abigail's daughters need to know that, if they're to know their mother at all.

Tuesday, August 18th

*

Pain today, not constant but uncomfortable. An uneasy reminder of how close it is and how much more there is to dying than being dead.

Today, too, I paid for my funeral. When Mrs Murphy called this evening, I gave her the receipt. I think she found that distasteful but she took it and said something about my courage. I laughed.

Wednesday, August 19th

*

No pain today. At all. I did tell Dr F, when he called this morning, that yesterday was bad. He insisted that I call him, if it recurs.

He told me, too, that he'll have word on Abigail's daughter on Monday. Which one, if any? And where?

I didn't work today, either. I dawdled down the canal and watched the children swimming at the lock and kept wondering about this woman that I want to meet. I picture a face and a house and a garden and I can't take it any further.

Thursday, August 20th

*

Another painless day so I returned to my work.

*

As ever, after something as alarming as your father's visit, we were conscious of the dangers to your mother's health but his arrogance seemed to have done nothing more than confirm her resolution to pursue her life and

*her faith. There were times of sadness and upset but she
refused to surrender to them.*

*She returned to Athy and Carlow the following week
and preached again. It wasn't that she had become blasé
about this task but rather that she believed it to be a part
of our mission and she was willing to undertake it, rather
than leave it undone in Joshua's absence.*

*

That isn't quite the truth. There were nights, three or
four, in the following week when Abigail couldn't sleep.
Nights spent in tears, when her talk bordered on the
gabbling that had filled her mind during her illness.

She'd cry and whisper about Lydia and Myfanwy and
then break down again and I'd hold her in my arms and
bury my head in the dark river of her hair and feel the
turns of her body against my own and I'd want her.

I knew nothing about lovemaking but I sensed what
I might do and I craved an opportunity to move from
the role of comforter to that of lover. Had the moment
come, I would have taken it. I wanted her mouth, to
taste her tongue. I wanted her eyes, to find assent in
them. And then I wanted her body, to explore and ven-
erate. But the moment didn't come. In those times she
was alone, forsaken, but the hope she clung to was the
hope of being reunited with Lydia and Myfanwy and
Joshua. All I could do was be there.

*

On the last day of August, I went with John Wickham to Athy for flour. After we had done our shopping and John had spoken with a number of people of his acquaintance, we set about our journey homeward, out on the road towards Levitstown, past Aughaboura and the Coneyboro and by the gates of Ardreigh House, a residence set well back from the road, its gardens secured by high walls. As we passed the gates of the house, I glanced in and could scarcely believe my eyes. Whether it was because of shock or uncertainty, I said nothing to John Wickham, but once we had rounded the bend that would take us onto the open road I asked him to rein in the horse and allow me to go back to look for a shilling I claimed to have dropped.

He willingly stopped the horse but I had to dissuade him from coming back with me. Once he had accepted my word that I could find it alone, I ran until I was out of his sight and then approached the recessed gate of the house, staying close to the wall so as not to be seen. I peered carefully about the corner of the gate but the drive and the garden beyond it were empty.

Had I been mistaken? Or hallucinating? Surely not? I had seen what I had seen. I didn't doubt my eyes or my mind. So I waited anxiously, all the time fearing John Wickham's appearance around the corner. While I waited, I foostered a shilling from my purse and placed it on the roadside before returning to my game of peep. And then my passing glimpse was confirmed. There, walking arm in arm with Catherine Devine, along the border of the lawn, was Joshua Jacob. They stopped here and there to smell the roses. Chatting, their heads bent close together, and then they moved along again. At the end of the lawn, they turned and strolled back the way they had come.

I picked my shilling from the roadway and ran back to the cart, hiding my shock and anger in a bluster about the search I'd made for the money.

I didn't tell your mother what I had seen. How could I? But I had to tell someone, so I told William. When he heard the news, his face fell like a stone.

'There may be a reason,' I said, though I already suspected the only explanation there might be.

'We know the reason,' William said.

He was silent for a while and when he spoke his voice was angry.

'We should tell the others, they should know.'

'No,' I said. 'No. Don't do that.'

'They have the right to know what is going on.'

'But we don't know what's going on ourselves, not really.'

'Hah!'

The sound was almost a spit.

'Let me find out more,' I said. 'Let me discover what is going on.'

'And how will you do that?'

'I don't know,' I told him. 'But let me try. Before we bring everything down in destruction about ourselves. Please. I was the one who told you, so let me find out.'

He sighed a deep, dark hopeless sigh and waved me away.

I was twenty paces from him when he spoke again.

'Were we cursed, Elizabeth? Coming here?'

I turned and saw that there were tears in his eyes and I went back to him.

'No,' I said. 'We were not. We came in faith and our faith will survive. And there may be an explanation.'

Should I have told your mother, broken the news then? There was no point, what could I tell her? That I had seen Joshua in the garden of Catherine Devine's house? What good would that have done?

I travelled by foot to Athy on the fourth day of September. The excuse for my absence was that I had arranged to meet my father and my English cousins and to spend some time with them. With money given to me by William, I took a room in the hotel and spent my time watching the gardens of Ardreigh House. By going down a slip lane to the side of the wall and forcing a small wooden gate, I was able to conceal myself in the rhododendron and watch the back door and lawns of the house. There, cramped, hot and hungry, I spent two days, from dawn to dusk.

On five occasions I saw Joshua walk in the grounds, twice alone and three times with Catherine Devine, and the ease of their closeness confirmed what I already knew in my heart. Their cosy laughter almost drew me from my hiding place. I wanted to rush across the lawns and confront them, throw your mother's trust and innocence

*in Joshua's face, shame them out of their self-satisfaction.
But I didn't.*

*As with so many other things in my life, I did not
respond to my feelings but weighed the matter up and
prepared myself when I might have been better off acting
on the spur of the moment.*

*

Sometimes, when I've most blamed myself for the times
when I wished Joshua out of our lives to have Abigail
to myself, I've consoled myself and mollified my con-
science with the memories of that day when I could
have gone back to Levitstown and announced his dis-
honesty to Abigail and the others but didn't.

*

*I stayed on in Athy that second night and sat most of it
in the corner of my hotel room, counting every tawdry
flower on the wallpaper, wrestling with what I should
do. I wanted your mother to know what was going on. I
wanted her to come with me, to see Joshua and Catherine Devine parading snugly up and down the lawn. I
wanted her to know exactly how things were, to banish
her illusions, but I knew I could not be the instrument of
such callous misery.*

*But was I to allow Joshua to use your mother so
lightly? He, like all of us, knew the terrible strain she
had borne in the half-year just gone. If he was insensible
to her loss of you, surely he was aware of her feelings*

for him? And if he had no intention of remaining with her, then he should at least have prepared her for his departure.

And what, I wondered, had brought about this transformation in his life? Was it the death of his wife? Had he been hurled into a maelstrom of depression? Perhaps, but my intuition doubted it. It was all too opportune, his long absence from the White Friends was too convenient. Try as I might, I abhorred Joshua Jacob for what he had done. He had allowed your mother to follow him, leaving her most precious loves behind. He had watched her go through grief and despondency. He had seen her court death. He had given her a sliver of trust and now he was prepared to risk her using that sliver to gouge out the hope that had taken root in her heart.

I became convinced, during that long, hot night, that neither your father nor Joshua Jacob cared a whit for your mother. They cared only for themselves. I do not say that all men were or are that way. William Ackworth and John Wickham were not of that ilk. Nor was George Carr, as I was to rediscover. Indeed, even James Stubb was a more honest man in his disagreement than either your father or Joshua. He at least acted by beliefs and not with only his own interests in mind.

And there was the difference. Those who cared responded to what was in their hearts. Those who were careless with the feelings, the very lives, of others were concerned with the mind. The mind is nothing, the mind asks why and where and when and how. It is influenced *by analysis. The heart understands compassion and fear and love, and responds to these feelings. It is consumed by desire.*

It has concern, that's the important thing.

I hope, wherever you are, that your lives are ruled by your hearts. I might have allowed my heart a freer rein but at least I followed it. And your mother followed hers, gave it the freedom of this world and the next. She was all heart. And I write that not as some trite cliché but in the knowledge that she lived and died by the tenderness of her heart, by the sincere passions that blazed inside her breast.

Friday, August 21st

*

Dr F. called this morning and told me that he has located Abigail's daughter. He doesn't know whether it's Lydia or Myfanwy but will know after the weekend.

'My contact knows her as Miss Beale. He doesn't know her well but it is your friend's daughter, I've garnered that from my research. The rest we'll know on Monday or Tuesday.'

I imagined I'd cry when I heard this news but I had no inclination towards tears. I was too happy.

'Does she know of me, of my search?' I asked.

He shook his head.

'But I'm sure she will, soon enough.'
When Dr F. left, I immediately set to work.

*

The first news that greeted me on my return to Levitstown was a letter from George Carr. He had written to William and enclosed with his letter was one to me.

I read it with pleasure and relief. He apologized for his sudden departure and assured me that he would come soon and visit us. He had settled at Fraughan Hill, just beyond Castledermot, and was no more than ten miles distant.

This news comforted me. I felt that my impression of him, my trust in him, had been vindicated.

His letter did not explain everything but, at least, it was a buffer between my own news and the dread I felt at telling it, even to William.

He received my account quite stoically.

'I expected this. I knew. You knew, before you went.'

I waited for him to rush into his tirade about the need to tell the others but he didn't. Instead, he asked my opinion.

'I think we should face Joshua,' I said. 'You and I. Before we tell the others. Before we bring unnecessary hurt. I'm thinking of Abigail.'

William nodded.

'And I'm thinking of the White Friends. I want us to stay together. We can do it, without Joshua. George Carr might return.'

'We don't own this house,' William said but, before I could reply, he added, 'But we can talk to Joshua about that. You're right, we should talk to him.'

I spent much of the rest of that day answering questions from the Fox sisters and Abigail about my assumed cousins and our supposed meeting over the previous days.

It was the following Monday, the eleventh day of September, before William and I managed to find an excuse to travel to Athy.

As William hitched the horse, Abigail stood with me in the yard, laughing, telling me that she was convinced William and I had fallen for each other.

'This is the start of it,' she giggled. 'Every chance you get, you'll be off together.'

And then she winked, a big, exaggerated wink.

'Enjoy it.'

I laughed, too, but it distressed me to think of the real reason for our journey.

On the short miles to Athy neither William nor I spoke much. We attempted to construct a line of questioning for Joshua but soon abandoned our attempt.

'Let him do the explaining,' William said. 'All we need to do is listen. Our presence there will be question enough.'

When we reached Ardreigh, we tied the horse in a shaded spot, across the road from the gate, and made our way up the avenue on foot. Our ringing on the bell was answered by a woman I had seen before, outside Athy barracks, in the company of Catherine Devine.

'We have come to see Joshua Jacob,' William told her.

She put us sitting in the marble-floored hallway and then disappeared inside. Minutes passed and we grew uneasy in the unfamiliar surroundings.

Finally, there were steps on a stairs and Catherine Devine entered.

'Yes?' she enquired, as though she had no idea why we were there.

'We're here to see Joshua Jacob,' William said, rising and towering above her, his voice crackling with starch.

'Then why have you come here?' Catherine Devine replied and her tone was every bit as stiff.

William laughed. It was not a sweet laugh and she was taken aback by its loudness and roughness.

'We know he's here,' I said. 'We simply wish a word with him.'

'You know a lot.'

'We do,' William declared. 'More than might be imagined. Now, we would like to speak with Joshua. We have wasted enough of your time and you of ours. Perhaps you would tell him we're here.'

'And who shall I say is calling?'

'Elizabeth Hallhead and William Ackworth, two White Friends.'

Catherine Devine disappeared along the corridor. William sat down again, a definite smirk on his face.

It was not long before Joshua appeared. I hardly recognized him. In the days since I had last seen him, he had shaved his beard and cut his hair.

'William. Elizabeth,' he said, bowing a little.

'We have come about the house in Levitstown,' William barked. 'We wish to make arrangements for its purchase from you. We wish to keep it as a home for those who are remaining in the White Friendship.'

'That can be arranged,' Joshua said.

'Good. Then perhaps we can discuss the details. We're anxious to allay the fears of those who are truly committed to the ideals of the White Friendship. They have lost enough without losing the roof above their heads.'

'There's no question of that.'

'Nothing is beyond question.' William smiled coldly. 'We know that well enough. We've learned that sometimes the words that are claimed as the words of God are simply memories of what God might have been about.'

'I don't understand,' Joshua said quietly.

'I believe you do,' William replied. 'Now, about the house?'

I understood William's hurt, his refusal to even acknowledge Joshua as a White Friend any longer, his anger at the sight of the man, but I wasn't prepared to let either of them forget Abigail.

'What you did was despicable,' I said. 'You used us and that was wrong but you abused Abigail Beale.'

'I have never laid a finger on Abigail, other than in tenderness and care.'

William's laughter split the air and he stormed out of the hallway and onto the avenue. I was glad because his *departure gave me the opportunity to tell Joshua exactly what I knew about his relationship with Abigail and to paint for him, in detail, a picture of what his neglect had done to her and what his running away would do to her.*

'I am not running away!' he shouted.

'No,' I told him. 'You're spending forty days in prayer and contemplation. You're less than four weeks gone from us and you're happily ensconced here. You've abandoned everything you were. And you've abandoned the woman who would live and die for you. And without as much as one word of explanation. You're a shabby, abject man.'

And then the tears began to fall. His tears, not mine.

'I've carried the White Friends since their inception. I've carried the expectations you all had. James Stubb wanted a Job of me, William wanted a Moses of me, the Fox sisters want a Saviour of me, John Wickham wants a home of me, you want an escape of me, Abigail wants a husband of me. I am the one who must find God and hear Him and be imprisoned for Him.'

'How dare you!' I screamed and my scream brought Catherine Devine running from one direction and William from the other. 'How dare you lump whatever expectations we might have had of you with Abigail's feelings. You haven't done her the courtesy, in four weeks, of telling her that you're living a handful of miles from her. How dare you throw her health, her mind, her heart, into your contemptible bonfire with the rest of it.'

Catherine Devine opened her mouth to say something but I wouldn't have it.

'And you!' I shouted. 'Do you have any grasp of what this wretch has left behind him? Are you aware of the torment and heartache he has caused? I don't believe you are and if you were, I don't believe you'd care. Carelessness is an awful thing because it will eat you from the inside out.'

'Leave us a moment, please,' Joshua said to Catherine Devine and she went.

'I have suffered,' Joshua said quietly. 'I did what I believed God wanted of me, I followed what I believed was His guidance, I did as I believed He bade me in founding the White Friends. I fasted, I prayed, I listened for His openings, I gave up my house and my business, I travelled and preached, I took on followers and found a home for them, I left my wife, I undertook to marry another in the belief that this was what God wanted, I challenged Friends and the law, I went to prison, I did everything that I believed God asked of me. I slept in ditches, went for days without food and water, in the belief that I was preparing myself for the word of God. I hurt my wife. I hurt Abigail's husband. I forsook everything in search of the truth and finally, when I had lost everything, I found something. A place where I could recover my sanity. A place where I could bind my wounds – not yours or Abigail's or anyone else's but mine. I found this place, this house. I couldn't go on because there is nowhere to go. I had nothing left. I went

into the wilderness and that wilderness was in my own head. I didn't believe any more. That was the greatest opening of all. I went away for forty days and I said I would return and I will. But I have nothing to bring but the word that I have no word. That's the only knowledge I have, after everything that has been done and lost. I'm here, with Catherine, because she doesn't expect me to carry her. She carries me. I can't carry people's expectations any more.'

'And what of Abigail's love?' I asked.

'That, too, is an expectation. She expects me to be the husband and the children she left behind.'

'You cur,' I said. 'You were the one who set yourself up as a Messiah. She followed because you led. And you leave her for forty days, preparing herself for your return. And then you talk like this.'

'I talk like nothing,' Joshua spat and something of his old tone returned. 'You hear what you expect to hear, as you always did, all of you. You lived in dependency. Take the house and the message and the belief and make it your own, if it is your own. If you believe in the White Friends then keep the Friendship alive. But you do it, don't saddle me with your expectations.'

'There's no point in talking to this man,' William said, as though Joshua were a stranger. 'All we can expect is to come to some agreement on the cost of the house at Levitstown. A rent of some description.'

'There's no question of rent. The house was bought in good faith—'

At the phrase 'good faith', William guffawed but Joshua completed his sentence.

'. . . was bought in good faith for the White Friends. It was never my intention that it should belong to anyone else. My wife put her money into it for that reason and it is yours to do with as you will.'

'We will pay a rent,' William insisted.

'Very well. The rent is one penny a week.'

William produced a half-crown from his pocket and handed it to Joshua.

'Thank you,' Joshua said stiffly. 'You have paid thirty weeks in advance. The next rent is due in May. Or thereabouts. I will send a receipt by the post.'

'Then our business here is done,' William said to me and he walked to the door.

I tried to catch Joshua's eye for I wanted something of him, some recognition of the fact that our business was not done, that there was a wall of pain to be faced. But before I could get his attention, William turned and spoke.

'One last thing, when you have finished thinking of your own great sacrifices, remember the rest of us who followed you. We didn't follow in the expectation of being carried. We came because we believed. And we go on believing. We gave up something, too. We all made sacrifices. It was just that you were too concerned with your own to notice the losses other people suffered.'

With that he descended the steps and I felt obliged to

follow but, halfway down the avenue, I turned and ran back to the door and hammered on it.

Joshua opened it.

'You must do something for Abigail,' I told him. 'You must. You cannot let her fall this way.'

'Elizabeth,' he said, and his tone was grave, 'in the beginning I tried to lift Abigail from her melancholy but I found myself being dragged down with her and if I continued to support her we would both have been lost.'

'She sacrificed everything to follow you.'

'I never asked her to give up everything. I showed her the light, as I showed it to all. If you followed, you followed for your own reasons. And so did Abigail. I did her no harm. It was she who made something of what was between us, not me. And the longer I was there the more dependent she became on me. I cannot cure her pain.'

'I could remind you of conversations you had with Abigail,' I said. 'But, doubtless, you'll remember them yourself. I hope you do. You know you were as much an agent in the love between you as she was. Or so you had her believe.'

And so I left Joshua Jacob. I knew I would see him again, it was my intention, for I did not believe he had accepted his responsibility to, at least, tell your mother of his decision to leave her.

Our journey to Levitstown was a slow one. We discussed how and when we should tell the others what had happened. We had two weeks before Joshua was expected and we agreed we should wait at least some days before making any final decision. And so it was. The days passed and, whenever the chance came, William and I tried to agree a way that we might break the news gently.

Abigail took our meetings as a further sign of a growing affection between us and teased me about it.

'Who knows, we may yet have a wedding before our own. We may even have a double wedding,' she said one night when she was full of talk and I was full of apprehension. I came close to telling her everything but I could not.

The more frivolous she became the more fearful I was. As I saw it, the greater her elation the further her fall would be. I tried to ensure that life was as mundane as possible. On this, William and I were agreed.

'Soon we won't have to pretend,' he told me. 'Our finances will see to that.'

Once, in the third week of September, I went alone to Athy and met with Joshua but he was as intransigent as he had been.

'I have told you why I did what I did,' he said. 'If you cannot accept my reasons then there is nothing further I can say to convince you. I know my own feelings, I cannot make you understand them. I will explain them to the others, when the time comes, and hope they are more willing to hear.'

'The time is coming on this Sabbath. The fortieth day of your absence.'

'I know that. This is my responsibility, not yours.'

'I'm glad you recognize that fact, Joshua,' I said.

He smiled, paternally.

'You never liked me, Elizabeth. You must be gratified that I have lived down to your expectations.'

'I followed you,' I said.

'But for your own reasons.'

I related the conversation to William that evening.

'It's time to tell the others,' he said. 'They should know before he comes knocking with his justification. They should be prepared.'

'Will you tell them?'

He nodded.

I put my hand on his sleeve.

'Sometimes I laughed at you.' I smiled.

'Did you?'

'I did. When you didn't wear your britches under your smock.'

He chuckled himself then.

'But you're a good man, William. You're kind and reliable and we'd be lost without you.'

'I'm no saviour,' he said, bleakly.

'We love you,' I said. 'And you've earned that love. Don't undervalue your importance to all of us.'

Saturday, August 22nd

*

Today would have been Abigail's eighty-third birthday. And I celebrated it in her presence!

I woke early, just after seven, but forced myself to stay in bed and, as I hoped, I fell asleep again and didn't waken until almost ten. I wanted that extra sleep because I wanted extra strength.

After a good breakfast, I set out to cycle to Castledermot, nine miles from here. It was a crisp, sunny autumn morning with a nip in the air. Ideal for cycling. I stopped in Kilkea and ate some fruit and then I cycled on. Mullaghcreelan Hill was steeper than I remembered and I rested, again, at its summit. And then it was a pleasant slope into Castledermot village.

The place has changed nothing in sixty years.

I found St James's churchyard very easily and left my bicycle at the gate. It was early afternoon by then and the sun had thawed the frost from the air.

That rambling, overgrown graveyard, stocked with stones that tilt and bow as time dictates. Such a beautiful place, a place I might have been buried but I surrendered my right to the comfort of such an intimacy a long time ago.

But today I put all such thoughts away from me. Today I was well, I was strong enough to get to Castledermot unaided and I was damned if I'd let my own regrets get in the way of this celebration. And celebration it was!

I've never forgotten the place where Abigail is buried. Sixty times in sixty years, on this day, I've found the peace to close my eyes and envisage that small parcel of ground. And each time it came clearly. So, today, I had no trouble in finding it, beside the stony ditch that divides St James's from the farm across the hedge.

There's no stone, no cross, just the barely perceptible swelling of a hummock. Abigail's grave.

I brought no flowers. I considered dahlias but decided against them. Once, thirty years ago, I saw sunflowers on a market stall somewhere in the Cotswolds and I thought how wonderful they would have been for her grave but there are no sunflowers to be found here and, anyway, she has slept without flowers for six decades so there's little need of them now.

So, I sat for an hour on a stone in the ditch and listened to the crows arguing in the trees overhead. I said nothing and allowed my mind to drain of both hope and regret. I was happy to be there. If there is a way of knowing these things then Abigail recognized my presence. And if there isn't, then at least I got solace and rest and satisfaction from the surroundings.

I didn't outstay my energy nor did I feel any melodramatic urge to look back. Instead, I stopped off at a café in the village and had a meal before setting off for home. Since visiting the undertaker, I've noticed a more practical bent in my character. Getting home safe and well and with some strength remaining was my main concern.

And I got back to Offaly Street just as the angelus bell was ringing over the town, tired but not exhausted.

It's been a very beautiful day. There's an immense peace in St James's and a great consolation. If anyone deserves that kind of serenity it's Abigail.

Monday, August 24th

*

Today was a thoroughly unpleasant one. I woke to the sound of rain on my window and was greeted by a grey sky that seemed to find the weight of the showers difficult to hold much above roof level. I took it as a sign that I might work all day. And so I've done. And what follows is an account of events that occurred on and about this day sixty years ago. How things seem to synthesize these days!

*

Joshua was due back in Levitstown on Sunday, the twenty-fourth day of September. On the previous Friday night, with my agreement, William announced that he wished to talk to us. The tone of his voice set everyone on edge, for it was obvious that he was nervous. As he cleared his throat, I saw John Wickham frown, in expectation of William's departure, I guessed.

'What I have to say to you doesn't come easy to me,' William stammered. 'I shouldn't be the one to tell it but Joshua isn't here. And won't be. Joshua went away from us almost forty days ago but he will not be coming back. He has left us, left the White Friends. That is what I have to tell you.'

He seemed surprised that everything was over and done in a matter of seconds.

'Has something happened him?' Abigail asked.

'No,' I said, for I felt that William had done enough in breaking the news. 'Nothing has happened. He's staying in Athy, with Catherine Devine. William and I have spoken to him. He doesn't wish to be a member of the White Friends any more.'

Between us, we tried to explain the circumstances of our discovery of his hiding place and our attempts to get some explanation of him. We were at pains not to hurt Abigail any more than she must be. But neither she nor the Fox sisters seemed to understand or accept what we had told them. They were united in their incredulity.

Ann Fox went so far as to laugh at our story.

'Joshua will be back. On the Sabbath or the day after. This is a jest.'

'Do you think I'd jest about something like this?' William shouted.

'It's his jest,' she said. 'You have been taken in by him. Wait and see.'

And with that she tripped off to her room, her laughter echoing through the house. Mary followed a moment later.

'It's not a jest,' I said to Abigail. 'We saw him, we talked to him, we heard what he had to say.'

'We can only wait on the will of God,' Abigail replied quietly. 'I have faith in God and in Joshua.'

'Don't hang your heart out for anyone,' John Wickham said softly, so softly that I felt myself go cold.

And then he smiled at Abigail and reached across the table and took her hand and held it. He looked tenderly at her before withdrawing his hand and going out into the garden. I knew that he believed us.

I followed him for I saw that he was in greater shock than your mother. I found him sitting among the vines. His back was bent and he seemed ready to sink into the earth around him. Tears were channelling the lines of his haggard face.

I knelt at his feet and said: 'It's not the end, John.'

'I think it is,' he said.

'William and I intend to stay here. Joshua isn't taking the house. That will be left to us. We'll stay.'

His eyes brightened a little and I smiled at him.

'This is our home, your home, this is the White Friends' home, that hasn't changed.'

He nodded.

'I hope so.'

That night, when we were in bed, Abigail refused to discuss things with me.

'If Joshua is in Athy, if he is troubled, then I am the one who should have spoken to him,' she told me. 'You know that. Now, I have no more to say on it.'

We woke the following morning to find that Abigail was gone. We guessed, immediately, that she had walked to Athy and William set off in pursuit of her. They returned at midday. Abigail had spoken to Catherine Devine, who insisted that Joshua had left.

'I believe he has,' William said.

'And he will return here,' Abigail added.

'I hope so,' I said.

Suddenly, her arms were about me and she was assuring me as she might a frightened child.

'Of course he will, believe me. Everything will be all right, Elizabeth. He will come. It may not be tomorrow, you know Joshua, he has always been a day or two out, that's the kind of man he is.'

And all that day and the next, in spite of Joshua's failure to appear, her optimism remained assured.

I was so confused at the time. Abigail was right, she should have been told. Neither of us had thought to bring her to Ardreigh House to see Joshua. We had treated her badly, given her no credit for common sense. In a way, I hoped Joshua would come back, I hoped it had all been a mistake. I couldn't deal with the unreality that surrounded us. The Fox sisters' disbelief; Abigail's blind faith; John Wickham's fear and the uncertainty that haunted William and me. It was truly a terrifying time.

Tuesday, August 25th

*

Dr F. telephoned this morning. His 'find' is confirmed.

I thought the news would set me on a frenzy of writing but it didn't. Instead, I spent the day rereading my account. Wondering, again, whether there's too much or too little in there.

And, then, wondering about Miss Beale. But which Miss Beale? And what kind of Miss Beale? Her mother's or her father's daughter?

And Dr Fullard's question about when I'd like to meet her?

She knows of the existence of this 'friend of her mother' and would 'very much like' to meet me. I wonder!

And, so, with the object in sight, I've spent the day doing nothing. Not writing a word. Using the excuse of rereading to avoid further work.

When do I meet her? Sooner rather than later. There's only sooner left to me! The weekend after next, I told Dr Fullard. If that suits.

'I'm sure it will,' he said. 'I'll check it for you.'

Something else has just struck me, I don't know where this woman lives. No name, no address. If I'd been as absent-minded all my life, how many households would have ground to a halt?

Wednesday, August 26th

*

Back to the grindstone.

*

In the week that followed Joshua's expected return, the atmosphere in Levitstown was grotesque. Work continued. Abigail even went to Carlow, accompanied by the Fox sisters and John Wickham, to preach. Neither William nor I had the heart to travel with them.

As they left, Abigail made one of her jokes about our being alone all day together but I didn't have the verve to feign amusement.

Neither of us could see a way out of this sad and futile circumstance. How long were we supposed to continue with the pretence of a pretence? And how long could your mother carry this expectation before it evaporated and left her with nothing to hope for and nowhere to go? I didn't know which was worse – the cloak of the moment or the daggers of coming days.

Ultimately, that predicament was resolved by Joshua Jacob.

The last day of September, a sallow and gauzy Saturday when summer and autumn melted into one in the orchard and across the stubbled flaxen fields, brought him into our yard. None saw his arrival and his knock

207

on the kitchen door was followed immediately by the shadow of his large frame bending through the low opening.

Abigail and the Fox sisters and I were in the kitchen. It took them an instant to recognize the clean-shaven, short-haired man before them.

Whenever Joshua had returned from his wanderings, he had arrived hungry, bedraggled, dirty and scarred but now he came in the full of his health, his skin glowing, his clothes immaculate.

He wore a blue shirt and a tweed jacket and corduroy trousers. No white smock. No indication of the garb we had all been instructed to wear. No outward sign of the man we had known.

Whether it was this superficial change or something else about Joshua's presence I do not know but Ann Fox fled through the door and only returned when she had found William and John and brought them with her. In the meantime, Joshua had seated himself at the table.

I believe his reappearance was a greater upset to Abigail than his absence had been.

Only when William and John and Ann arrived did anyone speak and then it was John Wickham's voice that fractured the unquiet stillness.

'Say nothing but the truth, in the name of the Lord,' he urged.

'I've come to speak the truth,' Joshua replied.

'Good,' John said.

'You've been told, no doubt, and you can see for your-

selves, that I am not the man I was. I have been through much in these last months. I've explained this to William and Elizabeth and I will explain it now again.'

And then he went into his talk about the weight and the responsibility and the need to find our own beliefs and to follow them. All the things he had said to us in Catherine Devine's house. When he had finished, it was John Wickham, again, who spoke.

'If you've left your beliefs behind you, if the White Friends no longer hold a place in your heart, does that mean your openings were not openings at all but the ramblings of your mind?'

'The White Friends do hold a place in my heart and always will,' Joshua replied. 'As for the openings, I believe I was not in health when they came to me. I no longer trust them, if that is what you're asking.'

'That is what I'm asking,' John said quickly. 'Everything is gone, then, everything you taught?'

'It's gone for me. When I was among you, I was turned in on myself. I have found a more open way since. But this may yet be your way forward. This may be your light. I cannot say this is not the way for you, how could I?'

After this, there was a prolonged silence which ended only when Joshua made as though to leave. Then Ann Fox spoke.

'You taught us much, Joshua, and you opened the way to the light. That cannot be undone. When you spoke of your openings there was truth in what you said. You

*were an instrument of the Lord's ministry. And will be
again. Your strength carried us and ours will carry you
until you come back to us.'*

*Joshua smiled and thanked her and then stooped out
the door and strode across the yard and onto the roadway, without a word to Abigail.*

*

In the moment of his leaving, I expected him to call her
after him. And I expected her to follow. I could think
of nothing but that night in the orchard when she lay
with him, begging him not to talk of love but to show
her love, and I forgot my own passion for her. I wanted
to run after Joshua, to drag him back, to beg him to
stay, to plead with him, point out that at least his presence and his talk of love were better than nothing, better
than the void his going would create in Abigail's life.

I could only guess at what was going through her
mind. I wished she would scream at us, release the anger
that must be in her but she said nothing.

*

*But it was she who was the first to react after he had
gone. Taking a cloth from the bar of the range, she began
to wipe down the crumbs from the table, bringing them
neatly together into her hand and then throwing them
into the open grate. It was such an ordinary, harmless
thing and yet there was an intensity about it, an ordi-*

nariness that terrified me. It was as though nothing of consequence had happened then or ever in her life.

Thursday, August 27th

*

The threat of September frightens me, as though changing the name of the month – rather than the day – will speed or slow anything. But at least I have my great crusade to return to.

*

The convention of that image, of your mother sweeping the crumbs into her hand, holds for the days that followed. We slept, we worked, we ate, we prayed. William tried to bring the conversation to the subject of our future but no one was willing to talk of it. Only when he insisted on discussing our finances did he get a hearing.

He reminded us of our need for money to see us through the winter. The garden had kept us in food for the summer and autumn but that would not last much longer. Firing and food were the immediate necessities. Our reserves ran to six pounds. We would not starve immediately but as the winter drew on we would have to find a way of supplementing our savings.

John Wickham offered to find work on a local farm

but William pointed out that John's work in Levitstown was much more valuable to us.

'Indeed, if we could find the money for a greenhouse you might feed us through some of next winter,' he added.

John's eyes lit up at the suggestion. 'That I could,' he laughed.

'Then we must find work,' Abigail said. 'Two wages coming in would make life tolerable. There must be work for us in Athy. I can do shop work, I know enough of shopkeeping. And you, Elizabeth, what do you know?'

I thought for a moment but nothing came to mind.

'You know gardening,' John Wickham suggested.

'Yes, I know something of gardening.'

'Then you could help John,' Abigail said quickly. 'And you, William, could find work. And Mary and Ann could continue with their housekeeping here. That seems a solution to our problem.'

'It does,' William replied. 'If we can find employment.'

'We can only find it by looking, so we will look.'

And so they did. And found it. William began, that week, to labour on a farm near Kilkea while Abigail was to work four days a week in a shop in Athy. In the meantime, she insisted on continuing our preaching.

'We can't hide away from the world,' she told us. 'We preached in the past, our preaching brought Ann and Mary to us. There will be others.'

So we travelled to Athy and Carlow where Abigail preached and Ann, Mary and I distributed our pam-

phlets. As ever, Abigail chose her texts at random and her preaching was more intense, more profound than it had been. It was as though she needed people to challenge her, to give her the opportunity to defend what we were about. And there were those who did.

On our second day in Athy, Matthew McAuley, the Elder whom we had crossed at the Meeting House, disputed with Abigail, quoting Deuteronomy.

'"Neither shalt thou commit adultery,"' he shouted, over and over.

When, finally, he hesitated for breath, Abigail said very quietly but very coldly: 'Will you be the first to cast the stone, are you without sin yourself? If you are, stone me here and now. I am ready.'

McAuley turned away, mumbling. Abigail returned, immediately, to the text she had been speaking on.

But McAuley would not be bested. He came back twenty minutes later with other Friends, several women among them, and they surrounded us, forcing us off the path and into the open gateway of a shop yard.

'You dare to continue this blasphemous behaviour,' he screamed, 'you who left your children for a man now installed in the bed of another woman! Have you not a whit of shame in you? Have you no feeling for your deserted children, no humility on their behalf? Are you intent on lowering yourself into the lowest gutter and bringing their infant names with you? Give up this whorish spectacle and go back home, or at least take yourself

off the streets before you are locked up in the lunatic asylum. You are senseless and reckless and an insult to the Friends who try to live a life in this town.'

While he spoke, we were driven further into the yard. I wondered whether the plan was to force us out of sight so that some violence might be done to us. It seemed likely, for McAuley's face was purple, his eyes glinting and dazzling, his mouth spitting. And the mob about him seemed as disinclined to Friendship as any I had seen.

Your mother, despite her bravery and her refusal to retreat in the face of aggression or harassment, was ashen. One hand clung to my arm, the other was spread in a protection of the Fox sisters. Back and back we stumbled until there was nowhere left for us to go, until we were trapped against a coach-house wall. The crowd around Matthew McAuley gave us no room at all and his face was pressed against Abigail's, howling and slobbering.

'Will you leave this town? Will you? Will you? Will you take your fornication and your blasphemy and your Satanic work and leave this town, will you? Will you take your coven of prostitutes and leave this town in peace?'

Had your mother wished to answer him she could not for his face was a raging, malicious eruption from which there was no escape. Had she tried to speak I believe McAuley's upraised hand would have come down on her

head and, had that happened, I am sure we would all
have been torn to pieces.

I don't exaggerate in writing this. There was hatred
and blood in that yard. Everything that had been bred
into those people was forgotten. Base human nature, not
belief or practice or doctrine, was raging in the confines
of those high walls. I was certain that our end had come
and that it would be both vicious and agonizing. The
moment had arrived and none could stop it.

I cannot do justice to our fear but neither can I do
justice to what followed. That voice. An ascension. And
the song which I had never heard before but would never
forget. I glanced to my left and saw Mary Fox, crippled
Mary Fox who seldom if ever spoke, her eyes closed, her
lips scarcely moving, and I knew that was where the
sound flowed from, surging above Matthew McAuley's
cawing, lapping gently against the walls of our prison,
washing the malice from the air.

'Love, oh love is sweetly flowing,
on its banks are lilies growing
and the waters are bestowing
love, love, beautiful love,' she sang.

She paused momentarily and there was silence but for
the sound of Matthew McAuley's breathing. And then
she sang again.

'Come ye children, freely gather,
learn to bless and love each other,
it will bind your hearts together

215

in love, love, beautiful love.'

Short as the song was, by the time it had finished McAuley's rabble had disappeared and he was left alone with us.

'You should go now,' Ann Fox told him when her sister had done with her song.

And he went. I almost felt for him. He had no answer when faced with the love he claimed to espouse. He was a wretched sight.

We escaped that yard and crossed the square to where our pony and trap were stationed behind the courthouse. As we prepared to leave, Joshua Jacob appeared, walking along the river bank. He saw us and came to where we stood.

'Are you well?' he asked with a hearty smile.

His question went unanswered.

'I hope you are well,' he said, a little less assured now.

'You will come back to us,' Ann Fox said. 'I know you will.'

' "And the angel of the Lord said unto her: Return to thy mistress, and submit thyself under her hands," ' Abigail said.

It was only later that I recognized the phrase from Genesis but Joshua obviously knew its source and fled from it, walking briskly away from us and across the Barrow bridge.

'He will come back,' Ann said, again.

And so, shaken and upset, we set out for Levitstown

and the comfort of John Wickham's garden and our own homely kitchen.

Your mother's experiences in Athy did not stifle her willingness to preach. The following Sunday, she went with William to Carlow Meeting House, and spoke there, too.

It seemed preaching had replaced everything else in her life. At night, when we were in bed, I tried to talk to her but she would not discuss anything beyond the mundane events of the day. She went to work on her set days. On her days off she worked in the house or preached when the opportunity presented itself. Sometimes the Fox sisters went with her and sometimes I was her sole companion.

Mary and Ann Fox had cocooned themselves in the belief that Joshua's absence was a temporary one, that soon he would return to us in some uncertain kind of glory and then everything would be all right. Their incessant talk was of what Joshua had said about going in leaves and the time when the leaves would fall and we would all be cleansed of sin.

'That time is coming,' Ann Fox insisted. 'This is the time of the falling of leaves, this is the time Joshua told us of, this is the time of his second coming among us, the time of salvation. We will be saved, he will return and save us.'

They took to collecting leaves and drying them. I took to avoiding them as much as I could for their talk was a recitation and I had heard it twice too often. And anyway, John and I were busy in the orchard, picking apples for winter storage.

Finally, one afternoon in the middle of October, while we were walking in the fields near the river, I managed to get some response of your mother.

I asked her straight whether she was as unhappy as I imagined her to be.

'I am the mother of the generations. How could I be unhappy? I am the voice of the White Friends. People listen to me when I speak in the streets. I have lost my children and I was twice a fool in love. I'm gone beyond unhappiness,' she said. 'I don't know where I am, or who, or how I exist but I do exist. Something keeps me functioning. I think it's the memory of my children.'

I didn't know what to say but I felt I must say something.

'We love you, Abigail. I love you. And William and John and Ann and Mary.'

She seemed to snap back, then, from the dreadful place from which she had spoken and her voice had a sudden edge again.

'Mary and Ann,' she laughed. 'Mary and Ann are deranged.'

And we began to laugh and we went on laughing until the tears flowed down our cheeks.

I enjoyed that time of giddiness but I knew it wasn't real and when, that night, after supper, Abigail asked Mary Fox to sing for her I knew that, too, was unreal.

Mary sang and we listened to the beautiful words again. John Wickham sat enthralled but I was uneasy.

I sensed something falling apart. Something had gone beyond repair and I saw that none of us could restore what had been. Too much damage was done, too much had been ventured and lost. I was despairing.

And when, the following morning, I walked outside and viewed the rusty, frosted dahlias and the cadaverous vines on their gaunt wires I was frightened. Everything frightened me. William and Abigail were away about their employments and John Wickham and I were striving against the grim winter earth. In the kitchen, Ann and Mary Fox waited on our illusory redemption.

I looked about me and my fear turned to terror. I recognized the eyes of despondency. I knew that everything was far beyond our control.

Friday, August 28th

*

Today I was too sick to work.

Sunday, August 30th

*

I had two injections yesterday and today the pain is bearable. Dr F. told me that the fifth is arranged. He'll drive me there. I told him that was a nonsense but he wouldn't hear otherwise.

'I'm every bit as intrigued as you are,' he told me.

I asked him which Miss Beale we'd meet and he didn't know. But he does know where she lives. In Tipperary town. We're to drive there for lunch on Saturday.

'Provided you're well enough,' he told me.

I will be.

Tuesday, September 1st

*

The month has crept in, in spite of me. I feel a good deal better but wrote very little today.

*

On the twenty-second of October, the second last Sunday of the month, Mary and Ann Fox disappeared early from the house at Levitstown. When John Wickham rose, just after eight, they were gone. They left a note, announcing that the day of salvation had come and that they were gone to meet the redeemer at Athy Meeting House.

William and I went, immediately, in search of them. We drove to Athy and found them walking through the town, dressed only in leaves which they had sewn together, and followed by a small but vocal crowd.

Our attempts to intervene and persuade them away

with us were hindered by those not willing to have their entertainment cut short. Mary and Ann processed through the streets and across the square and into Meeting House Lane. There, outside the still closed door of the Meeting House, they urged the people to prepare themselves for the arrival of the redeemer.

'He will come in the time when the leaves fall and his time is nigh and nigher,' Ann told them and they, in response, shouted encouragement.

Soon afterwards, Athy Friends began arriving, to be greeted by the two women, clad in leaves, standing in the yard of the Meeting House.

One of the Elders sidled by them and opened the Meeting House door. At this, Ann Fox shouted that the time had come, that we were saved, that we need no longer be ashamed of our nakedness because all sin was wiped away.

And, as she spoke, she and her sister tore the flimsy leaf dresses apart so that they stood naked before the braying mob.

With a surge, William broke free of the men who were blocking his way and pushed the sisters through the open door of the Meeting House, slamming it behind him. The crowd jeered and shouted for their return. A few children ventured into the yard and threw the leaves into the air. With that, the police arrived and the excitement ended. The crowd was pushed back along the lane, out into Leinster Street.

I made my way inside and found William and the

Elder who had opened the door with their coats wrapped about Ann and Mary Fox.

Later, they were taken to the police barracks and from there their father took them home with him, that afternoon, to Carlow.

We never saw them again but we heard it rumoured that Ann remained at home while Mary was sent to live with cousins in England. Another story ran that both were committed to the mental asylum in Carlow but we had other, more important matters on our minds and the manner and timing of their departure did not overly concern us.

Wednesday, September 2nd

*

My recovery continues, though recovery is the wrong word. The remission continues. As does the work. And the weather, a glorious Indian summer day.

*

I don't believe the Fox sisters' disappearance had any affect on your mother. Indeed, I hoped, with our community reduced to four and with fewer mouths to feed, the genuine warmth between John and William and Abigail and me would flourish and we would find the peace we sought.

And so it seemed. We laughed, Abigail and I, about the Fox sisters, and she asked me, many times, to describe, again, the events at the Meeting House. We didn't discuss the matter in front of William because he saw no humour in what had happened.

In the week following, Abigail and William went to work as usual. With less light and less need for me in the garden, I undertook the housework and cooking. I looked forward to the fall of darkness when John came in from the garden, to be followed in time by Abigail and William. Then we sat before the blazing fire and ate our meal and talked. Later in the evening, we told stories and read and prayed.

William had taken Ann and Mary Fox's room and I suggested to Abigail that she or I might take Joshua's but she preferred to continue sharing. As did I.

So the days passed. November came and winter settled in the fields and ditches. We prepared ourselves for the season. John Wickham oversaw the delivery of several carts of turf and wood. We had enough money to survive without too much hardship. We had arranged our lives between work, rest and preaching. Weekdays were spent in work, the evenings in relaxation and we agreed that on Saturday mornings we would travel to Athy or Carlow and preach there.

It was on the sixteenth day of November, a Thursday, that Abigail returned early from her work in Athy. I knew, when she stumbled through the door, that something terrible had happened. She sat curled by the fire, rocking and moaning and I could get no words from her. At first, I thought she had received word of some catastrophe befalling one or other of you but I realized that such news would have come to Levitstown for none of her family would have known her workplace.

John Wickham came in and he, too, tried to get some sense of her but could make no headway. He knelt beside her and she buried her head in his heavy coat and eventually sank to sleep there. He remained propped against the chair, refusing to move lest he wake her. That was the man he was. I may have said this before but he was the father she never had, the father she needed.

After William had arrived home and Abigail had woken from her exhausted slumber, we got some reasoning of her. Slowly, the story unfolded.

That afternoon, as she returned across the town, about some message for her employer, she met Joshua on the Barrow bridge and he told her that he had become a Catholic.

'He told me his time with Catherine Devine had shown him the folly of his ways. Her Christianity had taught him that all his travelling and searching was a journey to her home and the true faith.'

'If everything is so easily tossed away then let it be so for him,' William said.

Abigail seemed to recover somewhat then and she ate some food with us and I saw to it that she went early to bed.

But during the night her crying woke me. I enquired what was wrong and then she told me more of the conversation she'd had with Joshua.

'He urged me to go back and find my children. As though he didn't know how I've wanted to go back. As though he hadn't told me, time and again, that my sacrifice was sanctioned by God, that my suffering was a blessing.'

'I know,' I said.

'He told me we must all find new truths and some of us must go back to find them and some must move on. I stood on the bridge and I wanted to walk away but I couldn't. I felt I must endure this added distress, that I deserved it. Perhaps I do deserve it, Elizabeth.'

'Of course you don't,' I told her. 'You know you don't.'

'I had my chance to go back, when Robert came here. How can I now? How can I face the rebuff of being driven away again?'

'If you want to go back, I'll go with you. So will John and William, you won't be alone,' I said.

That seemed to ease her a little and she settled towards sleep again and then she said, very quietly, so that I wasn't sure if I'd imagined her voice: 'Joshua told me his truth is with Catherine Devine; they're to be married the last day of this month.'

If Abigail had been dismayed on hearing this from Joshua's mouth, I was every bit as shocked by the ease with which he had inflicted another cruelty on a woman who had never once wronged him and who had done everything he ever asked. A woman who loved him with a love he would never find again.

I was speechless. All I could do was put my arms around your mother and tell her how sorry I was. It was little enough but it was all I could do.

*

And a terrible need came over me that night. A need to protect Abigail, to show her love, to kiss and caress away her sorrow. I contained my emotion but I knew what I really wanted to do, how much I wanted to love her.

Thursday, September 3rd

*

I know I won't get this history finished, at least not to my satisfaction, by Saturday but I thought it would be wonderful if I did. So, I began work this morning, just after ten, with the windows wide open on another beautiful day.

I always valued the beauty of the countryside, rain or sun, and I'm glad of that now. How awful to try to make up for that in a few weeks!

*

Your mother appeared to recover from the her shock and for a number of days her spirits seemed to lift her out of her sadness and trauma.

We kept a close eye on her. John or myself, or both of us, went to meet her each evening from her workplace. I always dreaded the stretch of road leading to Ardreigh House. What if Joshua or Catherine Devine appeared? What would that set off in Abigail's heart?

But we saw no sign of them and on the last Saturday of November, the twenty-fifth day, we travelled to Athy, at Abigail's urging, and she preached in the square.

I was not in favour of such a journey but she was insistent. When I suggested Carlow as an alternative she rounded on me.

'Are we to run and hide from every shadow that approaches?' she asked, and I knew she was right.

But I doubted her strength to face Joshua or Catherine Devine at that time and it was her well-being that concerned me.

So, we travelled to Athy that day and she preached and we distributed our pamphlets, the last of the pamphlets that Joshua had had printed, as it happened. Afterwards, I thought there was a certain irony in that.

Of course, there was no sign of Joshua or Catherine and the afternoon passed peacefully, apart from a few taunts from men on the other side of the street who suggested Abigail and I should take off our clothes 'like your other women, the ones we want to see. Do that and we'll join you.'

As darkness drew on, we left the town and drove back home. I made a special meal that night and we sat late before the fire, enjoying each other's company.

If I tell you that it was a most peaceful night it is not to soften anything that follows, it is simply to assure you that there were periods in your mother's later days when harmony and quietness brought her a little tranquillity.

We retired about midnight and your mother was asleep before I was. I read on into the small hours and didn't wake until almost nine. I lay in bed awhile. Your mother was already up but there was nothing unusual in that. It was only when William came crashing into the room, calling me to come quickly, that I realized anything was wrong. I followed him, in my nightgown, across the needle-frosted yard to the shed where John Wickham kept his garden tools. John was already in the shed, attending to your mother, who lay shivering and convulsing in a corner. Her eyes were wide but she saw nothing. John held her until the seizure passed and then William and I carried her inside. By the time we had her in bed, John was already on his way to Athy for a doctor.

Abigail passed that Sunday and the next day in unconsciousness. The doctor assured us that there was nothing he or we could do.

'She's in shock,' he said. 'Sleep is her best medicine.'

On Monday night she came to herself and ate some soup and on Tuesday she was well enough to get up and sit by the fire.

On Monday afternoon John had set off, again, for Mountmellick, in the hope of persuading Abigail's father to come and see her. He returned on Tuesday, about the lunch hour, having gained an interview. He told your grandfather that Joshua was gone. He explained, once more, how tenuous your mother's hold on health was but it all came to naught. John was then a man of sixty but he undertook that journey at his own suggestion and without hesitation. We all owed him more than we could ever repay. We didn't, of course, tell your mother of his journey and she didn't notice his absence.

Her recovery on Tuesday morning was temporary. That evening she was restless and rambling in her speech. I tried to get her to bed, but instead she kept wandering into Joshua's room and looking through his books and papers, patting his pillow and mumbling to him in loving words that should have been heard by him but which were sad and tormenting to our ears.

It was obvious that she was becoming more and more distressed as the night wore on, and around eleven John Wickham walked to the house of Mick O'Connell, our nearest neighbour. He returned shortly afterwards with a half-bottle of home-made whiskey and he heated a glass of this, mixed it with sugar and cloves, and spoon-fed it to Abigail. In time, it had the desired effect and she became calmer. Finally, she drifted to sleep and we all went to bed, weary and worried.

*

But there's more that I don't dare to write to Lydia and
Myfanwy. More about that night. More about me.
Something I've never written down before. Even the
consideration of writing is difficult. As though putting it
on paper, even in this diary, makes it public. As it will,
to some extent, if I leave it behind me. Maybe that's one
purpose for everything. Not just to tell Abigail's daughters about her but to tell someone about me. My need
to confess may be a great part of this undertaking. Have
I written everything, just to get to the point where I
must write of that night or deny it? Knowing I can't
deny it? Maybe.

This is what happened.

I was woken sometime, about three or four that
morning, by Abigail's voice. Her eyes were open and she
was talking, not in the rambling, intense tone she'd used
earlier, but in a low, affectionate voice.

I'd fallen asleep with the candle still burning by the
bedside and now I could see the light reflected in her
eyes. I knew she saw me but I knew, too, instinctively,
that she didn't recognize me. Her words were perfectly
coherent but they were meant for Joshua.

'My darling,' she said. 'I want you to kiss me, you've
never kissed me enough. You've never been tender
enough with me. I need your tenderness. That'll make
me well again.'

She reached out and touched my hair and smiled.

'You love me, don't you?'

'Yes, I do,' I said.

'Tell me you do.'

'I love you, Abigail. I love you,' I whispered and I bent to meet her mouth.

I half expected her to recoil from me but her kiss was as eager in return. And then she began to pull off her nightgown, as she'd done for Joshua in the orchard. I made to stop her but she brushed my hand away.

'Don't be shy,' she said and her smile was crooked and mischievous. 'Let me see you.'

So I took off my nightgown and we lay side by side and I kissed her mouth and her neck and she kissed me, her tongue idling behind my ear, her hands holding me to her, her mouth inviting me to love her. I did. I can't deny that. I was the lover Joshua never had been. I kissed her and touched her until her skin shone like the kind of light you sometimes see in the sky at dawn. She was radiant. I closed my eyes and heard the pleasure in her uncertain breathing. Nothing breached our closeness, neither guilt nor fear. We were the lovers I'd dreamed but this was no dream. Our sweat was as real as our kisses and our pleasure. When, finally, we pulled on our nightgowns it was almost bright.

Before she fell asleep, Abigail touched my hair again and whispered a goodnight.

There. It's done and told.

If that had been another night, if what happened afterwards had been different, I might look back on my behaviour with some sympathy. But things weren't different and the guilt I feel is the same guilt I felt at that time. If anything, it has deepened with the years. I've told myself that what I did was done in the greenness of immaturity, that what happened happened out of love and longing. And that's true. And I've told myself that I did no harm, that Abigail was happy, that her waiting and frustration were swept away that night. And that's true. But I can never dispel the other feeling.

The feeling that her release, through our surrogate consummation of the love she had for Joshua, was also her delivery from the need for life. I had done what she needed done and I had seen her through the final gate, freeing her to leave it all behind.

I had bartered her need for my want.

Friday, September 4th

*

This morning, Dr F. called to check on me. I'm well today. I told him I'd hoped to have the account finished to bring with me tomorrow but I won't now.

'Perhaps it's as well,' he said. 'It'll give you something to bring to your next meeting.'

'If there is one,' I said.

'Of course there will be.'

'If the Miss Beale wishes it. She may not.'

'Who could resist your charm?' he laughed.

I suppose I could have made an enormous effort today

and tried to put everything into one last section but I was too keyed up about tomorrow, so I wrote nothing.

Instead, I took advantage of the continuing fine weather to walk to Ardreigh lock and back. The walk, as ever, brought me underneath the gardens of Ardreigh House. I remembered.

At the horse bridge, where the canal water eddies about Lord's Island, I listened to its applause as it fell into the sweep of the Barrow. A good omen, that joyous noise.

Sunday, September 6th

*

I was in no mood to write when we got home last night. How could I write on such a night? I couldn't sleep, either. I did take out the journal I've been keeping for Lydia and Myfanwy but there were too many things twisting in my head. So I waited till today to write them all down.

I was awake yesterday morning just after six and up, washed and dressed by seven. I did as Dr F. suggested and ate a good breakfast, in spite of myself, in spite of my terror. Like a ride I once took on a Ferris wheel in Leamington Spa. Terror and delight.

Dr F. was here at nine, as promised, and we set off for Tipperary, a county I had never visited. Driving there, I numbered the counties I've been to. Very few.

Kildare, Dublin, Carlow, Laois. Add Kilkenny and Tipperary yesterday. A handful.

The journey was more than pleasant. I felt safe with Dr F. He's such good company. We stopped at a little tea shop in Cashel.

'We've no idea whether this woman will even offer us lunch,' he joked. 'Better to arrive there fortified.'

The weather was exquisite and we drove at a comfortable speed. The sun warm, the morning bright. It seemed the leaves had stopped their turning. For those hours, moving through the countryside, I could believe that. Each time I enquired as to our closeness to Tipperary he put me off with some vague estimate.

And then we were driving into another town and Dr F. was slowing, searching for a roadway, swinging the car into an avenue between two houses, a long laneway that ended at a bungalow.

'We're there,' he said and he patted my hand as he got out and came around to help me out of the car. While I stood in the gravelled yard, he knocked on the bungalow door.

And then I saw her, coming from the garden at the side of the house, a slight woman, middle-aged but beautiful, dark hair swept back into a bun. And I said, out loud, because I couldn't help myself: 'Abigail.'

She smiled, the dead woman's warm smile.

'Not Abigail,' she said, quietly. 'Lydia. I'm Lydia, her daughter. I'm Lydia Beale and you must be my mother's friend, Elizabeth. I'm so delighted to meet you.'

I held out my hand and already the tears were pouring down my face. She hugged me to her and I smelled the smell of skin I'd loved, felt the gentle brush of that hair against my cheek, let myself lean into the succour that had never gone away but hadn't been real in sixty years.

Dr F. came back from the doorway and introduced himself and we chatted there for a few moments. Lydia insisted he should lunch with us but he wouldn't hear of it and made some excuse before driving away, promising to be back for tea.

I went with her and sat in her kitchen while she prepared lunch. Only when we were sitting over the meal did we really talk. I told her about Abigail and how we met and of the White Friends. She told me about her childhood, the little she remembered of Rosenallis and then moving to Tipperary and growing up there and never leaving, working with her father until he died, taking over the shop and running it herself until three years ago. She's sixty-three now but looks little more than fifty.

'And what of Myfanwy?' I asked.

'Myfanwy died in the influenza epidemic. She's buried here, in Tipperary.'

'I'd like to see her grave,' I said, remembering the two-year-old in her shining smock, in the shop in Rosenallis.

'Of course. I'll take you there after lunch.'

And she did. We drove through the town to the burial ground. There, she brought me to a grassed grave with a plain stone. On it were the name and dates.

MYFANWY BEALE
1897–1918

And below her name was another.

ROBERT BEALE
1869–1929

As we walked back to the car, Lydia asked if I knew where her mother was buried.

'In Castledermot,' I said. 'I was there two weeks ago. For her birthday. You should visit there.'

'I'd like that,' Lydia said and she began to cry and it was my turn to hold her.

When we got back to her house we walked in the garden and I asked her if she had a photograph of her mother. She shook her head.

'Do you?'

'No,' I said. 'But she looked so like you. The same hair, the same eyes, the same smile.'

We sat in a sunny corner of the garden, on a bench, and I opened my bag and took out an envelope.

'Thirty years ago,' I told her, 'I was working in a little village in England, Bishop's Tachbrook. One Saturday I travelled to Coventry and, passing a pawn shop, I saw a photograph in the window. It was in a silver frame. I bought it and gave the frame away. But I kept the picture because the woman in it reminded me of your mother. All these years I've kept that photograph, pretending to myself that it was Abigail.'

I handed her the envelope. She opened it and took out the picture and looked at it for a long time.

'She's a very beautiful woman,' she said, finally.

I nodded.

She made to hand the photograph back.

'You should keep it,' I said, pushing her hand away. 'When I saw it in the shop window, I thought it was a ghost picture, there for me to see. It was so like Abigail, it might have been her, the image. I think it was meant for me. And for you.'

And then I told her about my journal, my account of her mother's life.

'It may not please you,' I said. 'Some of it. I had no time for your father and grandfather. And I had no time for Joshua Jacob.'

'Who was Joshua Jacob?' she asked.

I explained as well as I could.

'We were told my mother had died when we were children. My father would stand in the shop, crying. I remember that, clearly. Years later, when he was dying, he told me she'd gone away when we were young and died in France. I never looked for her. It seemed a point-less task. But I'd like to go to Castledermot, to her grave.'

Dr F. returned just after five and had tea with us. We left just after seven. Lydia promised that she'd come and visit next weekend.

Driving home, Dr F. asked if I was relieved things had gone so well.

'Not so much relieved,' I told him. 'More, filled with pleasure. Joy.'

It was a joyous day.

I wasn't long home, and Dr F. had just passed me into Mrs Murphy's care, when the telephone rang. It was Lydia. To see that I was safely here and to thank me for coming down.

'I can't wait for next weekend,' she said and her voice sang with the eagerness of a girl. 'And thank you for the photograph.'

Of course I couldn't sleep last night. And of course I couldn't write. I find that hard enough today. But I will write tomorrow and through the week, to have the journal for Lydia.

I'm blessed with pleasure so late in life.

Monday, September 7th

*

This morning I made an appointment to see a solicitor. Another step! Otherwise, I set myself to writing Lydia's journal, for such it has become.

*

Your mother seemed to be more settled on that Wednesday, the first day of November. She slept through much of the morning and her sleep was peaceful. Both John Wickham and I looked in on her every half-hour. William was away at work.

Just before midday, John came in and sat with me to eat some lunch. We talked about Abigail and about our little fellowship. John was filled with brightness about our future.

'Come December, come the Christmas time, everybody's heart lifts. Then we won't feel the spring upon us. And after that the days bring their own happiness.'

'Where do you get such hope?' I asked. 'You're always filled with hope.'

' "What is my strength, that I should hope?" ' he said, laughing. 'If that unfortunate Job had hope then we should all have it.'

While we were talking, your mother came into the kitchen. She had put on her fresh white smock and, with her hair tied back, her skin had taken on the paleness of cloth. She was drawn but she was beautiful, too. She sat with us and took a little bread and soup.

Outside, the day was clear and sunny. A cold wind was coming in across the valley but in the yard, in the shelter of the sheds, there was some heat. After we had eaten, she went and sat there. John returned to his work in the garden and I prepared some of the food for our evening meal. When that was done, I went and chatted with Abigail awhile.

*

I wondered, as we sat in the sunlight, whether she had any recollection of what had happened the night before but she made no mention of it and nor did I. But I did try to be as close to her as I could, to touch her hair, to caress her cheek, to be loving towards her. Any contact was important to me that day. Any echo of the night before. And she looked so beautiful.

*

And she looked so beautiful.

'Joshua was right,' she said, after we'd sat in silence a time. 'This white smock is appropriate.'

Those were the last words she ever spoke to me, to any living soul, I believe. It was only afterwards I understood their full meaning.

I went back inside about one o'clock and baked some bread and tidied about the place. Now and then, I glanced through the kitchen window and saw her sitting where I'd left her. The last time I saw her alive, she was standing at the stone steps that led to the garden. I assumed she was going up to talk to John.

Afterwards, he told me he had looked across the yard from time to time and seen her sitting at the wall. And then she was gone. Just as I assumed she was with him, he assumed she was inside with me.

It was almost three o'clock when he came back into the house to make himself some tea. Seeing me working in the kitchen, he enquired if Abigail had gone back to bed. The fear that washed my face answered him and he immediately ran outside and searched the sheds and the orchard. I looked in all the rooms but there was no trace of Abigail.

'Maybe she's gone walking,' John said, to calm me. 'I'll take out the trap and go for William. In case we need him. Just in case. I'll ask Mick O'Connell to drive the Athy way.'

While John tacked the horse, I walked the road towards Carlow, to the first bend and then the second, telling myself I'd see Abigail around the next corner or at the end of the next straight stretch. And then I met a man walking from Maganey and asked him if he'd seen her but he told me he'd met no one on the road for three miles. I turned back to the house, hoping she was there, hoping we'd missed her in our search but the house was empty. It had that kind of emptiness that is unmistakable. The sense of nothingness was so strong in the house, and even the yard and the garden, that I knew it was all ended. And then the detail dawned on me and I set off, running, across the road, into the field and along the path, disguised by winter. But I knew that path and I raced along it, the stripped and battered whitethorns scratching out at me. Down the field and through the gap below the willows, where the frost always hid. Out onto the wide, bare bank, to the watery ash of the river, to the spot where we had all been baptized, where Abigail had given her heart and soul into Joshua's care.

And there she was, the plain, bridal white of her smock spread out about her in the sad, leaden waters of *the Barrow. I stayed only a moment and then ran back the way I'd come, calling all the time for John or William, but the road and the yard and the house were deserted. I ran to O'Connell's but Mick had already left. All I could do was wait on the road, straining this way and that for a sight of someone who might help.*

It was almost four o'clock when I saw John's cart on the road and ran to meet it. He and William came with me to the river and, while I watched from the bank, they waded in to take your mother's body from the water.

She was weighed down with stones bound into a sack tied to her waist. When these were loosed, her body floated like the leaves that showered slowly about us in the twilight. William and John brought her onto the bank. By then it was almost dark but the paleness of her face made a kind of radiance in the shadows of the over-hanging trees.

John Wickham went back to the house and returned with a wooden door. On this they carried your mother home.

*

Reading this back, I realize I was wrong in what I wrote. This is still Lydia and Myfanwy's story. And Abigail's. Theirs. And mine. Alive or dead.

Tuesday, September 8th

*

This morning, I visited the solicitor's office and made
my will. Not that there's much to will. This house and
furniture. My bicycle. My diaries. But I haven't included
those specifically. The account of Abigail's life will be
gone to Lydia by the week's end. So everything is done,
as swiftly and as plainly as that.

*

*I need not go into the details of our journey home. We
were met, as we came onto the road, by Mick O'Connell
and he helped with our pitiable task.*

*It fell to me to undress your mother's remains and
dress her in fresh clothes. And I did. I had never done
anything like this before but I did not balk at the task. I
was satisfied, if satisfaction had any part in that grim
duty, that it had fallen to me. I thought of it as Abigail's
last adorning and I was privileged to be there with her.
She had been companion and sister to me for nine
months. I had seen her go through a litany of doubt, loss,
torment, trust, desperation, faith and hopelessness in that
time but always she had been the one whom we loved
and whose love kept us together. I recognized that, as I
washed her body and dried it. I knew, as I dressed her
in a clean white smock, that nothing would be the same*

from then. Not because of her death but because of the changes her death would bring. I understood, as I braided her shining raven hair, that her loss would leave more than just an absence. None of us would evade the consequences of Abigail's going, our destinies were plaited into hers. I had no doubt about all this and, so, I made the most of my time. I was unhurried in dressing her. From the moment I left our room, I knew, everything would begin to come undone.

*

I hadn't at that time come to terms with my own loss, with the loss of the woman I loved. All that would come later. And did.

*

Word of Abigail's death spread through Levitstown and, by midnight the house was filled with neighbours come to pay their respects. They might not have shared our beliefs but were united in our grief.

William urged John and I to get some sleep, so that we might set off early the following morning for Mount-mellick, with word of Abigail's death and in search of arrangements for her burial. He and others from the neighbourhood sat through the night with her body.

Before I retired to bed, I went in, again, to our room, where your mother was laid. She looked so girlish, so beautiful and so young, so very young. In the candlelight,

I saw only the sleep of death on her face and nothing, yet, of its decay.

Next morning, John and I set out, as light was slitting the sky above Kilkea. We reached Athy before the day was fully broken. The town was deserted, our horse's hoofs rang back to us in the empty streets.

Passing along Stanhope Street, something made me glance across at the door of the Catholic church. Above its lintel was an arch of flowers, still fresh enough in the dewy morning. And seeing them I grasped their significance.

'Stop the horse,' I shouted at John and he did as I bade him.

I got down from the trap and crossed to the church door. By standing on my tiptoes, I reached the garland and pulled it down from the wall, scattering its flowers about the gravelled yard.

Climbing back into the trap, I felt obliged to explain my action.

'She told me they were to be married, Joshua and Catherine. It was yesterday. That's why she chose to do it, wasn't it?'

'That and probably too many other things we never knew about,' John said.

We journeyed on and, a long time later, he quoted, sadly:

'"Them that were bidden to the wedding would not come."'

We reached Mountmellick in the early afternoon and went, immediately, to your grandfather's house.

When we were ushered in he said: 'Why do you people persecute me?'

'We've come here because your daughter has died,' John said. 'That is a persecution but it's a persecution and a loss to us all. We've come to arrange with you for her burial.'

I cannot say your grandfather was unaffected. As before, I thought I detected a crack in his hardness but it was quickly recovered.

'You must bury your acquaintance as you see fit. It has nothing to do with me. Or mine.'

That last phrase incensed me.

'You'll damn in hell for this,' I screamed.

He nodded slowly and sank back into his seat.

'Good day,' he whispered.

So, once again, we journeyed home with nothing accomplished. My anger flared and blazed through every mile. John Wickham was silent.

It was night, black night, when we got home. Again, the house was filled with neighbours. William came outside to meet us and we told him our brief tale.

'Then we will bury her,' he said.

The following morning, he went to Athy and then to Carlow but none would accept Abigail into their burial ground. That afternoon, when he returned, we settled on digging a grave in the orchard, such was our desperation.

*But, as we talked, George Carr came through the door-
way of the kitchen.*

*He had heard of your mother's death that morning
and travelled from Fraughan Hill to be with us. We told
him of the circumstances and of the rejections that faced
us at every turn.*

'I cannot be certain but I may be of help,' he told us.

*He took his horse and left immediately. It was after
seven when he returned with the news that the Church
of Ireland rector in Castledermot, a man with whom he
had studied for the ministry, would find a grave for
Abigail in St James's churchyard.*

Wednesday, September 9th

*

This morning, a parcel arrived. From Lydia. Inside was
a record of overtures and intermezzi, which I've listened
to as I wrote during the day. *Cavalleria Rusticana* is
there, as are *Carmen* and *Samson and Delilah*. When I
visited her last weekend, I mentioned my love of music
to her but this was unexpected. However, being her
mother's daughter, I'm not too surprised. She simply
lives up to my expectations.

*

On Friday, the third day of November, 1899, we took your mother's body from the house in Levitstown, through Maganey and into Castledermot. Her coffin was placed in the back of a cart, driven by Mick O'Connell. William sat by him. John Wickham and I followed in the trap. Mick O'Connell insisted that he would not let a neighbour's funeral pass without attendance, in spite of anything.

It was about twelve o'clock in the morning when we came into Castledermot. Our passing drew a few stares but no great attention.

The rector had made arrangements for a grave to be opened and we arrived to find George Carr and two grave diggers there before us. The morning was clear and sunny but cold. We stood about the open grave and William spoke.

'We come here to commit the body of Abigail Beale to the earth,' he said. 'In her short life she gave much and lost much. May she find peace in the love of God.'

When he had finished, John read from the Psalms, his voice quiet but clear among the shadows of the stones, the huge round tower rising behind him.

'By the rivers of Babylon, there we sat down, yea, we wept, when we remembered Zion. We hanged our harps upon the willows in the midst thereof.'

Before John read this passage, I had been thinking of the verses in Samuel about Abigail, where he wrote that 'she was a woman of good understanding, and of a beautiful countenance'. And, as he read, I thought how appropriate the two passages were. But I didn't speak. Instead, as the gravediggers began their work I let my thoughts go with John Wickham's reading and I remembered Abigail beneath the willows at the River Barrow, the sun drenching us as we walked and talked and laughed. Such was the portion of her life that I wanted to recall then. There would be time enough, I knew, to recollect the other aspects, the days when she could hardly muster hope and energy to go on. And I thought of you, Lydia, and Myfanwy. I imagined you playing somewhere in the sunlight of that clear day, not knowing how much love you had lost, and I ached for you. For your deprivation and for the needless grief your mother had suffered and survived and to which, finally, she succumbed.

And as the gravediggers finished their work, I found my tears, the first tears I had shed since Abigail's death. We stood about the shut grave, loath to leave it, loath to walk away. I believe the feeling I experienced, while preparing Abigail's body for her wake, settled on William and John as we stood there. They saw that in Abigail's dying everything had changed for the White Friends, the Friendship had been buried with her.

And so it proved.

We returned to Levitstown and we remained there through the chill, wet days of November. Days when the darkness seemed to close in, not just around us but upon us.

And we were not there to see the Christmas hope that John had spoken of to me. Indeed, John was the first to go. He told us, one night deep in the pit of that dreary month, that he was leaving because he did not believe he could survive there any longer. We listened but neither of us queried his decision. We knew what he meant and how he felt.

When he left, the following morning, we knew he had gone to spend some time with George Carr at Fraughan Hill and we promised to keep in touch, but in our hearts all three of us knew we had neither the will nor the conviction to do so.

I think Abigail would have smiled at the thought of William and me, remaining alone in Levitstown. She would have blessed our condition and urged us to make a virtue of our necessity. Sometimes at night, lying awake in the room that had been our room, I imagined her urging me to settle down with William. And it might have happened.

A week after John had left us, William broached the subject of our future.

'We might stay here,' he said. 'But it would take a good time to build the Friendship again. Or we might stay here ourselves.'

I did not immediately respond and he returned to the subject a while later.

'We must decide what we will do. If we don't decide, nothing will come of anything.'

'And what are the choices?' I enquired.

'We can try to rebuild the White Friends or we can

settle here and live our own lives. But that would require a change in our condition.'

I smiled at his convoluted overture.

'Are you suggesting we would need to marry to stay here together?' I asked.

'Yes,' he said, quite matter-of-factly.

I laughed, the first time I had laughed in weeks. Not at William's proposal but at the way he had made it. And then he started laughing himself and much of the tension and dejection of that time seeped out of us.

We slept that night, a solid sleep that had not been possible for many weeks.

The next day, William brought up the question of our future there, again.

'We won't marry,' he said and I knew it was an acceptance rather than a query.

'Not because I'm not fond of you,' I assured him. 'But it isn't the way.'

'And do you see a future for the White Friends here?'

'Do you?'

He shook his head.

'I don't have the heart for it. If John Wickham is brought down by all of this then there's no hope.'

So, on the first day of December, a month after your mother's death, William and I went to Athy, and informed Joshua Jacob that we would be leaving the house the following week. He said little, other than to *wish us well. He never once mentioned your mother's name nor did he acknowledge the fact of her death and we would not demean her life by speaking of her in his presence.*

Thursday, September 10th

*

I was up at the crack of dawn this morning and started, immediately after breakfast, into my journal. I want to be sure the story is here for Lydia when she arrives tomorrow evening.

*

William said goodbye to Levitstown on Tuesday the fifth of December 1899. He, like me, had decided to return to his parents' home before making any further decisions.

Our parting was uncomfortable. We had grown to be close friends over that year and I was sorry to lose his friendship and he, I think, regretted many things: the collapse of the White Friends, the loss of so many companions and, dare I say it, the frustration of his affection for me.

He was a deep and grave young man and the end of the Friendship was probably hardest on him, for he was the one most committed to its ideals and practice. It was he, despite his doubts and reservations, who had kept us together through the confusions and changes of the preceding months.

We stood at the gateway, the horse snorting between the shafts of the trap, and neither one knew what to say. Ultimately, there was nothing to say. So, we hugged and I helped him up onto the trap and watched as he drove away, towards Maganey and Carlow. At the bend in the road, he lifted his left hand and waved but without looking back at all. And then he was gone. And, as with John Wickham and George Carr and James Stubb and the Fox sisters, I was never to see him again.

He did write once or twice, in the months that followed, but then I moved to England and we lost contact.

That afternoon Joshua Jacob came to get the keys of the house from me. I had arranged that my father should collect me the following morning. I wanted to spend one last night in the house. I hadn't told William of this, for he would have stayed to keep me company and that was not my design.

Joshua arrived about half-past two. Catherine Devine was with him but she stayed outside. I insisted on having him check that everything was as it should be, bringing him through the empty rooms, the beds stripped and tidy.

At the door, I handed him the keys, all but one, telling him that I would be leaving the next day.

As he was about to leave, I asked him, quite coldly, whether he blamed himself for Sarah Fayle's death.

'There's no value in blame,' he said. 'You will learn that.'

And then he was gone.

I stayed that day in Levitstown. I wanted to be there, alone, in order to say my own goodbyes.

In the faint, dreeping afternoon I walked up the garden, between the bare vines that would grow wild, if they grew at all. Fog dreeped from their spindly branches and knitted the spider webs between the wires. The fruit trees in the orchard could not muster one leaf between them. And the only sound was the cawing of the crows in the high trees about the ditches.

I walked back down the garden, into the gravelled yard. I stopped into the sheds, one smelled of turf, the other of the apples stored along the shelves there.

In the mist of the fading day the house looked long and low and cheerless. And inside my steps echoed across the kitchen and through the rooms. I wished I was away, wished I'd asked my father to come that day instead of the next. I trifled with the idea of lighting a fire but I didn't. Instead, I went into the room, our room, and lay on the bed without undressing, lay there all evening and through the night, drifting in and out of sleep until the dawn came.

I sat through the morning, waiting for my father's arrival, and when he came I locked the door and walked away without once looking back. Passing Mick O'Connell's house, we stopped and I gave him the key, said goodbye to him and drove away, without regret but carrying great sorrow all the same.

*And that is the story, our story, your mother's story,
Yours too, in part.*

*

So the work is done. Five months it's taken me but it's
done. I have something to give Lydia tomorrow. And
that was why I did it.

Saturday, September 12th

*

Lydia arrived yesterday afternoon and, after tea, I took
her for a walk down the river bank and showed her
Ardreigh House. Coming back I brought her by the old
Meeting House and the square. Then, when we got back
here, I gave her the journal and left her to read it while
I went to bed.

This morning, she told me she'd read it through at
one sitting and she thanked me for it. She said it meant
so much to her, to have this account of her mother's
life, to help her get to know the woman her mother was.

I was touched by that.

In the afternoon, she drove me to Castledermot and
we visited her mother's grave.

'Maybe I should put a stone here,' she said but, later,
she told me she didn't think so and I was glad. Abigail

is more at home in the shadows of the trees and the shelter of the falling wall.

We spent tonight in talk. Going back over many of the things I wrote about in the journal, answering her questions.

It was a sad day but complete.

Sunday, September 13th

*

Before she left today, I told Lydia of my own condition.

I think she was disconcerted at the mention of death. After she'd gone, I felt the energy drain from me. What did I expect now that everything is done?

Wednesday, September 16th

*

These have been bad days, I've lain in bed, not having the energy to get up, not wanting to. Dr F. has been several times, and Mrs Murphy is fussed about me, but I can't say I feel more ill. I have no pain, just this terrible tiredness.

Thursday, September 17th

*

The summer continues with such determination! Lydia has telephoned several times and is coming again to visit tomorrow. Mrs Murphy tells me I must be up and about to meet her. 'To bring her someplace cheerful.'

Saturday, September 19th

*

I was up to meet Lydia yesterday.

This morning we went out driving, through Ballitore, where I showed her the house where I was born, and on to Moone and back to Castledermot, where we stopped at the graveyard and visited Abigail's grave. Sitting there in the sunshine, picnicking among the very quiet dead, Lydia brought up the subject of my illness. I explained it all as well as I could.

As if to prove a point, I was quite sick on the journey back to Athy and Dr F. was called here and gave me an injection which made me sleep through the evening.

I woke about nine and chatted for a while with Lydia and Mrs Murphy but I feel quite tired and nauseous.

Sunday, September 20th

*

I slept late – the effects of the injection. Dr F. called just before lunchtime. In the afternoon, I sat with Lydia in the yard and ate a light meal. I told her I've left this house to her. She was genuinely astounded and made all kinds of protests but, as I pointed out, there is no one else I want to leave it to. I have no family and I regard her as such. The furniture will go to the Murphys, to keep or sell as they wish.

I wanted to tell her more, to explain how much I loved her mother and was in love with her but I couldn't find the courage.

She left, still protesting, still telling me to reconsider but, as I said, she's her mother's daughter and I'm happy in what I've done. I don't expect her to live here but the sale of this place may make her life a little more comfortable and that would please me.

Tuesday, September 22nd

*

On Sunday night I was ill again and Dr F. came twice in the night to see me. Yesterday, I was heavily sedated and couldn't keep my food down. When he called last night, I asked if this was it but he laughed and said I wouldn't be finished off that easily. I'm glad he has such faith in my resilience!

Today I was a deal better.

Lydia telephoned to enquire if I'd come down to visit next weekend but I told her I didn't believe I'd be able.

Thursday, September 24th

*

I'd love to have gone to Tipperary for the weekend. A break from here would do me good.

Would not do me good, rather would take my mind off everything.

Thank God for the long summer, I may yet be buried in fine weather.

Saturday, September 26th

*

Very sick through Thursday night and Friday. I asked Dr F. if this was a reaction to everything, to finishing my journal for Lydia, to meeting her. He said he thought it was and that I needed to set myself some other plans now, not to let everything go with what's gone. He suggested I set my sights on the visit to Lydia, to staying there for a few days. Maybe but I don't feel up to it.

She telephones every night.

Sunday, September 27th

*

Lydia arrived, unexpectedly, this afternoon and stayed till almost ten. She talked about her father a lot. She was anxious to give me a glimpse of the man she grew up with and stayed with all her life. She says she's sure he regretted not being kinder to Abigail. And having to live with the lie about what happened to her. Or so Lydia believes. Even now, I don't see that. I think back to his last visit to us in Levitstown, his brazen assumptions. But I said nothing. I couldn't agree but I didn't disagree.

Again, when she was leaving, Lydia spoke about the house, saying she found it all uncomfortable.

'It's you or the cats' home,' I told her. 'And I've never been too fond of cats.'

At the door, as we hugged, she gave me a copy she'd had made of the photograph I bought in Coventry.

'I think of this the way you do,' she said. 'As a picture of my mother. I know how important it is to both of us so I want you to have a copy, too.'

Monday, September 28th

*

The weather has started to turn. This morning was cool and thick with mist that didn't lift until well past eleven.

Tuesday, September 29th

*

Dr F. called. He's increased the strength of my tablets but at least I'm still able to get up, though I find it difficult to read, my concentration goes.

Wednesday, September 30th

*

Oh Lord, what a day! This morning, I went out to the yard to the line. It was about ten o'clock and the sun still hadn't broken the fog. As I was hanging the clothes, I turned and my face was caught in the dank fingers of a misted cobweb. It horrified me. It was as if I was back in the bakery, hearing the undertaker's voice for the first time. It was a tap on the shoulder, a ghastly reminder.

All day, I tried to get it out of my mind but it refused to budge. I listened to my music tonight but that didn't drive it away, either. Probably nothing will. There'll be other prompts and intimations as death comes to meet me. Its steps will grow longer and more assured, as mine become more tentative. I dread that thought.

Friday, October 2nd

*

I've made two decisions. Lydia is coming to visit tomorrow, and if I'm well enough I'll travel down and spend a few days with her in Tipperary. Mrs Murphy has me packed and Dr F. has me painless and bewildered with tablets. He says it's to ensure that I don't back out and to make me enjoy myself. I believe his motives are more pharmaceutical than that but never mind. I'm not in pursuit of pain.

We're into October now and the days and time are shortening, not just because of the season but I feel it in myself, in my own body. Despite what I thought and what Dr F. tries to convince me, this isn't just a reaction to finishing my journal for Lydia.

I've tried to focus on other things, like this visit to Lydia, but my condition isn't improving. And won't. I recognize that fact.

I don't want this diary to become the garbled and

witless rambling of a decaying old woman. It's October and it's time to let go. So I'll visit Lydia and I'll enjoy what may be enjoyed but I won't write in this diary again. That's one decision.

The second is more perilous and I've given it a lot of thought. I'm going to give this diary to Lydia, this and the other sixty-nine I've kept through my life. I don't expect her to read them all but I will ask her to read this. Not the journal entries that I've copied but the other parts, the parts I wrote for me. About Abigail. The parts that get inside our lives. Our life.

She should know the worst and best of what I wanted for her mother and myself.

I'd been toying with the idea for several days and then last night, late, around midnight, I was sitting here in my study, reading back through things I'd written thirty years ago. The night was mild and the window was open and I heard two women in the street, laughing. I caught a snatch of their conversation. One was telling the other about some man who'd been chasing her all summer.

'I wouldn't give in to him,' she said. 'I wanted to but I wouldn't and then last weekend we went drinking and he fucked me while I was drunk.'

And she laughed uproariously.

I think, Lydia, those women were faltering angels sent for me to hear. To remind me that I made love to your mother once, when she was drunk or close to it. I want you to know this: I regret the circumstances but not what I did. I wanted to do it, more than anything in my life, because I loved Abigail more than anyone in that life. I need you to know that, no matter what. She was all I wanted, yet I took advantage of her. But I believe she has forgiven me.

I wish there was something profound that I could write to finish this, something to ease any discomfort or distress you might feel in reading it, but I can't find anything that's adequate and I don't seem to have the energy any more to look beyond the obvious. Perhaps it's because I have nothing more to say. If I need forgiveness, forgive me, but try to understand me.